SEAFOAM AND SHADOW

SONG OF THE BLACK SEA

BOOK ONE

MYRA DANVERS

GLOSSARY OF TERMS

A quick and dirty guide to the monsters, moans, and mythology of the Black Sea

Pelagorn

A species of what modern-day humans would describe as 'merfolk', the Pelagorn are descended from deep-sea leviathan bloodlines. Apex predators born to rule the seas, evolved to conquer all oceanic environments from the trenches to the wandering open waters. Known for their bioluminescent scales, venomous anatomy, and feral instincts, the Pelagorn have ruled the seas, uncontested for millennia.

Virelii *(Female Pelagorn modern-day humans might call mermaids)*

The daughters of the tide. Elegant, ruthless, the Virelii is a term of deep respect for the mothers of their bloodlines. They are merely female Pelagorn.

Abyssari *(Pelagorn Subspecies)*

The abyssal race of deep-sea *Pelagorn,* who once ruled the

ocean trenches, but now dwindle in number, edging toward extinction. Born to endure the pressures of the deep, they sit apart from the other Pelagorn subspecies, and have conquered all of the ocean's deepest waters—*except for the Black Sea.*

Thalassari (*Pelagorn Subspecies*)

The oceanic, open-water race of *Pelagorn* who rule from temperate coastal waters to the frigid Arctic, they are the undisputed rulers of the seas, and after winning an ancient war against the *Abyssari*, impose strict regulations on their trench-born cousins that have pushed the deep water species to the brink of extinction.

Trident

A sacred weapon wielded only by an Abyssari-born king. It channels ancestral memory, war rites, and the power to command both reef and current.

Raskoril Coral (*The Black Coral Strain*)

A parasitic strain of coral cultivated from the blood and venom of Nyxarion Korrides. Engineered in exile from remnants of extinct *Abyssari* coral genomes, Raskoril was incubated in the anoxic trench of the Black Sea to serve as the foundation of Nyxarion's seat of power. Fed a steady diet of Nyxarion's blood and venom, it is indentured to his genetic imprint and responds to the will of its creator. Unlike traditional reef systems, Raskoril does not require sunlight or warm, coastal waters. It thrives in the poisoned, oxygen-depleted depths, feeding on whale-fall, detritus, and any hapless *Pelagorn* too foolish to keep their distance...

Knot / Knotted / Knotting

A biological quirk of the *Pelagorn* anatomy humans are not equipped to endure. To ensure a successful breeding even in ocean currents, a *Pelagorn* male will lock inside a *Virelii* after ejaculation. The base of his penis swells after climax, anchoring him inside while the breeding takes place. The pair then drifts through the current as mating concludes—sometimes as long as hours as they wait for the male's knot to deflate.

Sirens

Once human females before they were taken by force or sacrificed to the sea. They are transformed by venom, bred to carry the spawn of their *Pelagorn* mates, and birth a species of *Pelagorn* that can endure in the harshest of climates and introduce new bloodlines.

The Resonance

A powerful, ancestral frequency unique to all *Pelagorn* subspecies. The Resonance manifests as a deep, subsonic purr carried through the water, capable of stirring dormant polyps, commanding venom-reactive coral, and summoning deep-sea species from across the trench. It is neither speech nor sonar—rather, a biological vibration capable of turning sand to liquid. It is a sound Humans cannot hear, but one that compels obedience when turned upon a potential mate.

Caelith Mare (*The Seat of the Thalassari Throne*)

The legendary underwater capital of the *Thalassari*, Caelith Mare is the open-water stronghold from which Thalos rules over all Pelagorn subspecies. Built at the junction between the greatest oceanic currents of ancient, living coral reefs, the city is hidden in the heart of the open ocean. It serves as both a political seat and a religious sanctum, enforcing the Accord of Nisyros that now bans the creation of Sirens. Its influence stretches from temperate coastal territories to the Arctic ice shelves—every trench, tide, and deep-sea kingdom is subject to its decrees.

Threnakar (*The Seat of the Abyssari Throne*)

A mythic fortress sunken in the Tonga Trench in the South Pacific, Threnakar is the ancestral seat of the *Abyssari* throne. Carved from volcanic rock and a genetically modified, parasitic coral reef, Threnakar is a living monument to the deep. Surrounded by an active volcanic subduction zone, it was once a seat of unfathomable raw power, shrouded in bioluminescent glow, but is now crumbling and derelict. Accessible only to those capable of surviving the crushing pressure of the deep, it is said the throne itself remembers the bloodline of the kings who once ruled there. A relic of the Pelagorn war between *Thalassari* and *Abyssari*, its coral architecture breathes, pulses, and obeys the sovereign will of its true heir.

Vorynthar (*The Seat of the Black Sea Throne*)

Forged in defiance of Threnakar's memory and Caelith Mare's oppressive rule, Vorynthar is the living fortress grown by Nyxarion Korrides, last of the Abyssari kings, and first Sovereign King of the Black Sea. Nestled in the depths of the Black Sea, Vorynthar is a heretical reef, bioengineered from the forbidden strain of coral known as Raskoril, it is fed on the venom and blood of its sovereign. A fledgling seat of power, it is a young reef shaped to cage Nyxarion's drowned Siren bride and serves as an engine of life where no life should exist. Oxygenating the anoxic waters of the Black Sea, it is a claim of dominion and a living incubator for the next evolution of sea-born life.

Accord of Nisyros

A post-war treaty ratified by the *Thalassari* following their ancient victory over the *Abyssari*. The Accord of Nisyros established rigid laws governing the conduct of all *Pelagorn*, but most severely restricted the trench-born *Abyssari*, who started the war. It banned the forced creation of Sirens, outlawed cross-species mating, and stripped the *Abyssari* of sovereignty over their ancestral trench kingdoms. This treaty has begun their slow extinction by starvation, isolation, and regulation—while the *Thalassari* crowned themselves the rightful kings of all oceanic dominions.

vii

CANTICLE OF THE DROWNED BRIDE

I am Kore Dionari, of the divine flame. And I am the chalice.
My body the altar.
My blood the sacrifice no god wants.

But you, son of Poseidon, I feel you in my veins.
I feel you in my marrow, Beast.
Staining my womb.

You are the tide.
And I was meant to break across your cock.

I am the chalice.
Yours to break.

So drink.

PSALM OF THE SOVEREIGN KING

*I am Nyxarion Korrides, first Sovereign King of the Black Sea, and I
am the tide meant to drown the flesh of the sun.*

My voice the current.

My venom the storm.

My knot the anchor that binds you to the sea—where you belong.

*I am the tsunami that fills your womb. The toxin in your veins. The
plea to the divine your gods refused to hear.*
I came when you were alone. Found you hollow and made you whole.

I am inside you now, my sweet Siren bride. My living flame.

Mine.

You will break.
And the sea will sing your name.
So drown...

DEDICATION

Dedicated to every reader who's ever gagged at "moist," recoiled at "bulbous," and noped out at "slick."

Your suffering is my muse. May this book haunt your ick list forever.

And to the deranged miscreants who live for stories that throb with viscous heat, drip with an unspeakable slurry of all things briny, and howl for linguistic war crimes...

I abused the shit outta the English language. Just for you.

CHAPTER 1

They said the gods could be appeased through prayer. Sacrifice.

That Apollo's wrath might be soothed by spilling a few precious drops of vestal blood upon his sacred altar. Splitting virgins on the holy pricks of the priests made mystics by Apollo's divine touch.

They'd promised her sacrifice would protect the holy city of Delphi from destruction.

But the Oracle hadn't lived to see the city burn.

And now Kore knew the touch of a man *and* the taste of human ashes.

Shifting, she pressed her back against damp wooden boards, pulling a quiet hiss between clenched teeth as her sodden, dank little world tilted violently to the left. Her every movement echoed by a metallic clink of shifting chains as she slid to the end of her tether.

War.

It was as foreign to a priestess of Apollo as it was beloved of Ares. The women of her temple were called on to bless a hunt. To sanction new buildings. To fight disease, not… not *Athenians*.

Shivering, Kore tucked tighter around herself and stared into the gloom as everything shifted again. To the right. Rocking to a nauseating rhythm older than the gods themselves.

Delphi would be rebuilt. A new Oracle born and named so the Spartans might worship at Apollo's altar and throw their virgins across his mighty cock.

None of it mattered. Not to the survivors huddled in the hull of an Athenian trireme as it skated through the waves, left to cower beneath the surface of the Aegean Sea. In the dark. Sprayed by salty filth as it dripped down from the decks above.

It didn't matter to the women who'd been taken—the Spartan army wouldn't march for a handful of soiled priestesses who'd already given their maidenhead to Apollo. Worthless women whose blood hadn't been enough to save the holy city.

Sold.

The cry of the auctioneer still echoed in her head, even after these long weeks of hard travel.

Her worth was weighed in silver now.

Precisely two hundred and sixteen drachmas.

Scarcely more than six months' wages for a skilled Athenian carpenter—the man with a heavy paunch and ruddy cheeks had told her so. Bragging as rough fingers had speared between her legs. Probing at dry flesh as his apprentice inquired about her use and lifted her breasts to gauge their weight. Desperate to know when he might afford such a luxury as a personal whore. If he might use her himself, or if he should save his coin for one of his own.

The shock of it all had grown… weary. Beaten down by cruel hands and dulled by the passing of time, unmarked by the sun.

Now, all she could muster was a measured puff of breath. The only sign of discomfort that marked her among the living.

Most of the other priestesses chained to the base of the mast were too quiet to muster even that.

A distant shout brought her eyes up. Where faint, flickering light could be seen between the boards of the rowing deck, and thundering feet darted back and forth as a panic ignited above.

The ship juddered as if struck. Groaning with the weight of the waves, she tried to buck back to the surface.

Clutching at her chains, Kore fumbled for purchase. Trying to ground herself, even now. So far from the soil of the only home she'd ever known. Already half swallowed by the Aegean.

Above, the rowers made a valiant effort to push through the storm. She could feel them gaining momentum with each pulsing lurch forward.

Her fingers twisted in the familiar pattern she'd been taught when calling upon Apollo's grace.

But Apollo had forsaken her.

And Delphi's ashes had blocked out her last chance to glimpse the sun before she'd been dropped into the hull and forgotten. Cast out. Thrust into murky shadows flickering in the deep.

Frigid fingers twisted in a new pattern, then. Hesitant. Desperate. Calling on a different lord to deliver her from suffering. More powerful. Ancient.

For a moment, the ocean calmed. Soothed, as if listening. The only audible sounds were the clinking of chains, oars thrusting through the surf, and the ragged, wet breaths of the few living captives still huddled in the dark.

And then Kore's world exploded.

CHAPTER 2

*H*anging from her wrists, Kore screamed. Legs flailing, she thrashed wildly. Kicking at nothing…

… until her feet struck at something cold. Wet.

Water.

What had once been the floor was now the ceiling of her dark, tormented little world.

The ship had capsized.

The only screams she could hear were those of the slaves still breathing in the hull. Those few living souls also dangling from the base of the mast where they'd been tethered. Crying with helpless panic as the air grew ever more damp.

The ocean was gushing into the void beneath them. The ship was taking on water faster than she'd thought possible. Already, what had only teased at the tips of her toes had seeped well past her waist. Leaving her simple robe wet as it clung to her chilled flesh.

The Aegean was a temperate sea. Warm, when the sun might kiss away the chill.

But the water suckling at her nipples was frigid as it swallowed her body and took the bulk of her weight off her wrists. A terrifying relief that brought no comfort.

"I—I call to you, b-bright Apollo," one of the priestesses stammered. Her voice a clear bell in the dark. "S-Son of Zeus. Gentle-natured—" She shrieked, the sound a ragged assault on Kore's ears in tight quarters, only growing tighter.

It was a prayer she knew well. One for inspiration and grace. Meaningless here, where the son of Zeus could not see them and held no power.

Not after Kore had called on the mercy of another.

Even the air was heavy now. Tight and oppressive as the Aegean pressed in from all sides, forcing a great volume of air through tiny cracks in the ship's hull.

Kore closed eyes that saw nothing but dark shadows. Pulling rapid, terrified breaths through chapped lips. Quick as she could. Savoring every last one, because—

Crack!

A violent shudder shook Kore's entire world.

It rippled through her chains, rattled her bones, and made the water splash up over her head for just a moment. Sloshing and gurgling as if ravenous for another sacrifice—just one more—before she surfaced. Gasping foamy seawater into her lungs.

The mast.

It had struck the ocean floor with enough force to shatter wood like brittle clay. She saw the damage in a flash of distant, dim lightning. Splinters of wood longer than her torso embedded in the walls of the hull—and a hole torn clean through three decks.

"Save us!" the priestess beside her screeched. "Great Apollo—"

"Swim down!" Kore snarled, kicking against the weight of her chains as the water gushed into their prison with ever-greater speed. "With me! There's a hole—a chance! Our only hope of escape!"

She reached, legs burning with the effort to keep her head

above the surface. Trying to touch the other priestess. The only one she might save, if there was any hope at all.

But she was gone.

Taken by the waves without a whisper of protest or further complaint.

Chin tilted back, legs tangled in fabric, Kore took three final breaths. One after the other. Enjoying the taste of the putrid air, for it might be the last she ever sipped.

And then she sank.

Hands following her chain back to the mast, she guided the links over smooth wood. Blind in the dark. Ignoring the many other chains and the bodies attached to them, Kore let the weight drag her down. Saving her air to preserve what little strength remained in her muscles, she sank as if she were just another body sacrificed to the sea.

It was nothing to slip through the ragged hole between decks. Easy to find where the mast was broken clean in half. Claiming the end of her leash, Kore wrapped the length of her chain around her forearm and let herself sink further still.

Lungs not yet burning enough to force her final, soggy breath, her knees buckled when her feet struck the ceiling of the rowing deck. Blindly sweeping, she found the next gaping maw the mast had chewed through the ship and stepped through.

Her feet touched sand.

Sharp, uneven stone.

The squish of human flesh no longer warm with the fight for life.

A corpse.

Priestess or slaver, she couldn't guess and couldn't see. But they were all the same in death.

She pushed the body aside and crouched. Slender enough to slip through the gap between the ship and ocean floor, she kicked and fought. Clawing her way free of the ruined vessel.

The pressure changed around her in an instant.

The ship.

It was shifting.

Rocking with the force of the waves above.

Moving while she was still pinned between a sandy reef and what was left of the hull.

Panic bled through her veins, and with one final, mighty effort, she kicked and clawed. Scratching her way free—

It rolled in the sand. Unmoored. Refusing to let even one survivor escape this watery grave.

Kore was crushed.

Screaming, agony splintered through her legs and belly. The crack of her pelvis echoed in her ears from inside, the sound distorted and too loud beneath the waves. It rumbled through her bones, inside her skull, and drowned even the sounds of her screams.

She was doomed.

Lost, where no one would ever be able to look for her. Lungs empty, body broken, Kore's lips parted on that final breath at last.

A flash of lightning struck.

Her world was ignited by Zeus' might for a single, glorious instant. Enough that she saw.

Bodies, everywhere. The men who'd burnt Delphi and desecrated Apollo's priestesses now floated all around her. Some caught in the mooring, others torn to bits among the remains of the mast. Still more swept away by a relentless, ravenous current that would scatter their remains across the sea floor.

All of them dead.

The ship that had been her prison for weeks had been obliterated. Torn asunder when she'd struck a reef with fatal force, the Athenian trireme was broken in two uneven halves. Her remains already spread as far as that split second allowed her to see.

Darkness returned in a flood, and despite the agony of her horrific, imminent death, Kore summoned a smile.

Because she was grateful to Zeus for such a gift. To see her enemies brought low before she went to Hades for her final journey through the mists of Eberus to be judged.

Giving herself to the waves, Kore's eyes fluttered closed, one last time.

The cold no longer chewed at her marrow.

She was warm, as if submerged in a bath. Engulfed in delicious pressure that touched every ache, soothed every wound.

Dying was hard, but…

… death was… peaceful.

Easy.

When Hades came for her, it was with a firm touch. Hands with strength enough to pull her free of the wreckage, his grip wrapped around her waist. Looped beneath ruined legs that were dragged through sand without a whisper of protest.

Cheek pressed close to smooth muscle, she felt it when the Lord of the Dead commanded her to, "Yield."

So she did.

CHAPTER 3

Something warm was pressed to her lips.

Blunt and alive.

A divine libation that tasted of the sea.

Brine so sweet and full of vigor she couldn't help the smile that spread across her lips.

She drank.

Greedily.

With reckless abandon. Allowing herself to be fed, she was limp. Paralysed, anchored to the sands from the weight of her chains as ambrosia washed over her tongue and sweet currents drifted all around her. Caressing her hair, toying with the rags still clinging to her chilled skin. Playful now, as if it wasn't that very same current that had killed her.

He tilted her head back, repositioning that vessel behind her teeth. Driving it deeper, one strong hand wrapped around her nape, moving her into a position of servitude so she might accept more.

A tiny sound escaped her, then. The barest whisper of life still clinging to her mortal shell, she tried to refuse. Tried to gag and reject even as he pried her jaws apart and forced it deeper.

It was too hot. Too vibrant.

Too… *much.*

"Swallow."

It was a word spoken through the sea. Echoing all around her —through her blood.

A thing not heard, but felt.

It was a command she could not ignore, for he pressed the nozzle into her throat and pumped that glorious brew straight down into her stomach. Forcing her to drink the sea dry. Filling her belly with breath and warmth until she bulged with it.

Swollen and full.

When he'd fed her all there was to give, he pulled the spigot from her throat and ran thick fingers over her lips. Caressing. Almost… gentle. Tender, just for a moment before those fingers grew cruel. Tangling in her loose tresses, finding a firm grip against her scalp, he hauled her up from the sands of the sea floor and began to swim. Moving as if he were the ocean itself.

Pure, raw power rippled all around her. Every movement sent a current roaring behind him. Each heave of muscle moved the Aegean and parted the sea.

Towing Kore by her hair with one hand, she was weightless in his wake. She felt no pain—not even from her crushed legs and pelvis.

There was only… a glowing.

A cauldron of bubbling warmth in her belly that pressed against the walls of her abdomen, sloshing against her spine and organs, where she was bursting at the seams.

It filled her with ambrosia. Saturated her lungs with life and freed her from the pain of drowning, of being crushed by the full weight of the deep. But she wasn't breathing. Not really. She was… suspended.

Because she was already gone.

Hades himself had come to escort her to judgment, for surely only one of divine blood might swim with such effortless speed? Such elegant, powerful grace.

Kore didn't fear death, and she already knew suffering.

Already, she was intimate with the anguish of loss. And there was something… beautiful to be found in surrender. Something akin to freedom in trusting her devotion to the divine.

Clumsy, desperate for a glimpse of the Unseen One, Kore tried to lift her eyelids when something rough and sharp brushed against her cold skin. Tried to watch that which was forbidden from mortal eyes, to witness the moment the veil was lifted and the next great journey began.

All she could muster was a flicker. A tiny twitch of heavy lids that allowed her a hint of iron chains trailing behind, reaching down into the deepest dark. Fluttering rags that whispered and danced around slack limbs as the current twisted and thrashed around her.

In her peripheral, a flash of sparkling color undulated to her left in time with his mighty, sweeping kicks. A mirage she couldn't quite grasp with the barest hint she'd seen from the corner of her dead eyes.

But she saw the blood.

A slow trickle oozing from torn flesh, she watched a swirl of crimson even as it was washed away. Her skin cleaner than it had been in… weeks. Purified by the very waves that had killed her.

Her lids fell closed. Stinging. Too heavy to fight the blackness for another moment, she succumbed to the rhythm he set. Hypnotized by the flashes of beautiful glittering color, by the pulse of seawater thrust aside with every heaving kick. Listening to the song of the ocean as it sang a dirge for the countless lost.

The forsaken.

When he broke the surface, the night struck her with a cold slap.

She blinked.

Head lolling, breath still in her chest, she was dazed. Staring at a sliver of the moon hanging high in the dark sky above. An endless void speckled with countless stars.

A wave sent her rolling, and her eyes fell upon a shore. Close. Closer than she'd imagined possible, for this wasn't the Aegean sea, but a river. The waters tasted sweet and fresh, almost absent the salty tang of the Aegean.

Kore frowned, for this was not the path she had expected Hades to take to reach the realm of the dead. Every scripture she had ever read mentioned the entrance was located in Cumae... but... what might one mortal *really* know of such things, even if she'd been a priestess of Apollo?

She'd died at the bottom of the Aegean with hate in her heart, absent any coin to pay Charon to ferry her across the Styx. An improper burial, her last thoughts were vindictive. Filled with loathing for those who'd dare tarnish holy women. She'd been *deeply* pleased those men had suffered and failed before they'd been swallowed by the sea.

She'd died impure.

Dread bubbled behind her frozen heart, then. Enough to make her thrash against the unyielding grip in her hair. Trying to beg forgiveness. To plead with the Dark One to absolve her of such petty, ugly thoughts.

Ready to throw herself on his mighty bident, to bleed for him and prove herself worthy of everlasting peace.

Squirming, she tried to draw breath and found her lungs stiff. Too full. Refusing to expand, deep under the thrall of whatever he'd pumped down her throat.

He took no notice and didn't slow.

Ignoring her weak thrashing, swimming ever forward, he made light work of the river. Charging headlong into the current without pause. All through the night, he dragged Kore in his glittering, mysterious wake until the moon slipped behind the distant trees and the sun threatened to poke through the gloom.

And still, she couldn't twist far enough to see what was forbidden to her.

She felt only the scrape of rough flesh rubbing against hers as he powered through the current. Saw only the sparkle of a fabric so pretty, she'd never even imagined such a thing might be possible.

Hours dragged by, but still, she was all but frozen. Her lungs stiff and quiet. Her legs and arms fluttering in the current as he moved them through the night and into the morning.

Numb from scalp to toes, she hardly felt it when her chains caught at something on the river bottom.

Couldn't make a sound when she was jerked from his merciless grip and plunged beneath the shallow waters once more.

But she could see.

Pinned to the sea floor, tethered by those accursed chains chaffing her wrists raw, Kore spun with a violent twist.

For a moment, she couldn't make sense of the shadows. Saw only swirling water frothed by titanic effort as he reversed course to reclaim what had been wrenched from his control.

There was an instant held immobile.

A split second of pause that saw him lit by the dim glow of the distant sun. A halo of silvery, watery light that showed him for what he *really* was.

And then her gaze was drawn away.

Rejecting what her eyes so clearly saw, she looked instead to the spear in his right hand.

For clutched in that mighty grip, she saw his spear and knew the truth. That what she had assumed was Hades' mighty bident bore not two…

… but *three* prongs…

CHAPTER 4

angled in chains at the bottom of the river, Kore blinked.

Trying to deny what her eyes claimed to be true.

Eyes bulging from their sockets, hair floating in a dark mass around her face, she stared. Awestruck by the man... the... *inhuman* beast commanding the very current that ruffled her rags and caressed cold flesh.

Without thinking, she let her fingers twist in an unfamiliar pattern.

Calling not on the lord who had forsaken her...

... but on his uncle.

Again.

Just as she had in the filthy hull of the trireme. Repeating the exact same betrayal of her sworn lord, for floating above her wasn't a son of Zeus.

Or Hades.

But the son of Poseidon.

Triton.

In his right hand, a mighty, three-pronged trident gleamed in the dim light of the crescent moon. At his hip, a conch fastened in place with twisted weeds and braided shells.

But it was the demi-god himself who'd forced Kore's jaws to grow slack in awe. Her lips parted on a gasp that died before it might even be born, for her lungs were full of… him. Still frozen and unable to draw breath.

Heavy bands of muscle laced an impossibly broad chest. Ridges and valleys sculpted by an endless battle with his natural element, he was a behemoth. Undeniably male, yet where her brain insisted there should be a narrow waist above his hips that blended with thickly muscled thighs, there was…

Something else.

Scales.

Glittering and hypnotic. A seamless blend between man and leviathan, his tail was… *magnificent*. Thick with power, longer than she was tall, and ridged in fins that flicked and shifted as he held his pose above her in the current.

Letting her look.

A sound moved through her, then.

Something born from the Deep, for it needed no breath to live. Felt through her blood, moving through her bone and sinew, it was impatience and hunger. Derision and eager thirst.

It was *him*.

His voice. It filled the waves and conquered the surf.

With a single sweep of that mighty fin, he flipped and plunged through the depths to reclaim her. Hand outstretched.

She couldn't help but cringe.

Flinching, she flung her hand up to cover her face in some vain attempt to protect herself.

Merciless fingers found an anchor, engulfing her forearm from wrist to elbow. He hauled her up. Tore her free of the rocky snare where her chains had caught on the riverbed before he turned again.

Toward the surface.

Making short work of the depths, he carried on swimming without so much as a backward glance at his captive. Heedless of her weakening struggles, her silent pleas went unheard as he towed her toward a destination only he seemed to know.

Lungs frozen as if truly dead—neither breathing nor drowning—she dozed for a while, if one might call such a stupor sleep. Hypnotized by the way her limbs fluttered in his wake.

Senseless until the hint of fresh water had grown salty once more, for he'd used the river as a bridge to claim access into yet another sea.

One Kore couldn't name, for what use had a servant of Apollo for knowledge of geography? She'd known nothing but the shores of the Aegean. Never been anywhere but the temple of Delphi, where she'd served since she'd been given to the priests as an unclaimed orphan.

The next time they surfaced, the sun's rays were being swallowed by the night—the second such evening she'd spent in his company. As his tribute. His... captive.

And as she looked, the last of the sun's rays burned across the surface of the water.

Kore squinted and cringed away from Apollo's kiss... for she was unworthy of his golden touch.

Tarnished by a son of the Deep who'd come when she'd begged to be saved.

Rescued, but for what, she didn't know and couldn't ask.

She was helpless but to observe until the moon was high and they had arrived at last.

The demi-god slowed before he stopped.

Pausing only to observe the low tide before he surged forward once more.

Navigating the turbulence of the shallows with confidence and patience, he skirted jagged rock, eased over sandy banks, and dragged her through shallow pools warmed by even this weak sunlight.

Careless of her tender, water-logged skin, he dragged himself onto land. Using his magnificent tail as leverage, he moved with a slow, serpentine grace that was an insult to his mastery of the sea. It was ungainly. A chore to heave that heavy appendage across land and drag her ashore.

Kore's chains rattled across stone worn smooth by the endless tempers of the ocean.

All she could do was endure.

Ignoring the burn of tender flesh, she forced herself to grow deaf to the many unanswered questions echoing between her ears.

Contenting herself with prayer, she waited as he worked. Watching until he'd found a perch tucked beneath a rocky ceiling, he pulled her into a shallow cave. One carved straight from stone over many long millennia.

It was dry enough, she supposed, with the tide at its lowest.

A cavern that would flood when the moon was full and the waters high.

He turned, then. Dumping her in a messy heap of limbs and tattered rags and chaotic heaps of untethered chain, he watched her for a moment. Mighty chest expanding as he fought for breath outside of his natural element, he kept her glued to the stone with a fierce, alien scowl.

And then he lifted his trident.

Poised to strike.

Silhouetted against the sun, he struck a figure that might have sent Kore screaming for the safety of this unnamed ocean once more, could she so much as draw a single breath into frozen lungs.

As it was, all she could do was squeeze her eyes shut and wait. Blinding herself to the end.

When the trident fell, it struck with an impact that cracked stone. Sent shards of limestone to spatter against her bare, water-logged shins.

She yelped.

The first sound she'd made since emptying her lungs at the bottom of the Aegean.

A tiny scream none but he might have heard, but a sound nevertheless. One she was alive enough to make.

She blinked.

Blinked again.

And then Kore's gaze flicked to where the prongs of his trident were buried in the stone—and saw the true target of his strike.

Her chains.

Twisted metal was all that remained of the cuff that had bound her wrist to the base of the mast. The only remaining sign of her bondage to Athenian slavers was little more than a puddle of mangled scrap.

Forcing a tiny, ragged breath, Kore pulled air between numb lips. Trying to offer thanks. Trying to apologize for her doubt.

He yanked his spear from the stone as if it were nothing to do so, and turned once more. Shifting back to the ocean with deliberate, undulating twists of his tail.

Flinging one hand out, clumsy and inelegant, Kore tried to scream for him to wait. To beg that he not leave her stranded here, with no food. No voice. No water that wasn't poisoned to one not born to it.

All she could muster was a wet, wordless rasp.

It did nothing to slow him.

On he went until he'd reached dark, lapping waters once more.

Helpless, she watched as he slipped into the waves and was gone. Too weak to stand, too numb to explore, she curled around herself and set her head against the pile of linked chain.

Gazing up at the sky as her lids grew heavy with the need for sleep, Kore simply worked to breathe. Luxuriating in her ability to do so, each new breath was bigger than the last. Her ribs stretching and moving with proof that she still lived, despite it all. That she'd survived against all odds.

Her chin dipped as the battle was lost, sinking toward her chest. Where rosy pink nipples were pebbled against the cold, half exposed in the tattered remains of a ruined shift that bore the mark of her service to Apollo. The left one poked through, fully exposed, as if pointing an angry accusation up, toward Olympus.

And then she saw it.

A strange blue glow.

Dimmed by her rags, brighter where the skin of her upper belly was exposed to the chilly night air, it was a glow that came not from her skin…

… but *within*.

CHAPTER 5

$\mathcal{A}$gony sent him back to the deep.

His tail flicked at the surf, just once. A single powerful sweep of muscle and sinew that sent him down through the shallows. He drove forward into the great, crushing silence of the poisonous waters, muscles protesting with every heaving thrust.

Exhausted after the hard miles he'd invested in this girl. A broken slip of a human female. Disgusting creatures. Fragile and slow.

And yet, he'd towed her through hostile waters despite the cost or the risk. Wrestled rivers with currents strong enough to test even his resolve. And now, at last, she was marooned in the heart of the Black Sea.

Trapped.

He let the weight of the trident drag him down, his grip unrelenting while the rest of him went lax. Sinuous as he bled into the belly of the trench below.

It was a canyon. A crack in the sea floor yawning wide enough to swallow an entire human city. Deep enough to crush pretty surface things into a pulpy mist.

And totally anoxic.

Hostile to all life.

A tiny, eager smirk touched the edge of his lips.

Most life.

He prepared to fill his lungs with the last few breaths of oxygen-rich water as he dove into the poisonous layers. Slowing his heart, readying himself to seal his gills against the searing, acidic waters he'd find at the bottom, he snaked past cliff walls that dropped sharp and jagged in the gloom. Sheer black basalt dusted in silt, untouched for eons, for the current here was mild.

Cold.

Lifeless, to all but the untrained eye.

No kelp beds swayed here. Not a single flourishing reef teeming with life.

There were only volcanic vents chugging away into the gloom. Vomiting up noxious black clouds of boiling, mineral-rich water unfit for all but the most extreme forms of life.

Mats of festering bacteria, but little else.

It was hostile. Raw. Barren and unyielding. Hideous and uninhabitable. A place so toxic that his father had refused to colonize it and rejected every attempt to plan around it.

It was the closest thing he now had to a home.

Sweeping down, aggressively driving deeper into hostile waters, the ache in his joints eased. Replaced by a blistering fury that warned of damage to his lungs that only grew with each heaving breath of brine he pulled over his gills. Chest compressing the deeper he descended, he took as few breaths as he could stand and let the trident drag him down as he conserved his energy. Dropping until he could see the bottom of that cursed basin.

He took his last breath and entered the deadly anoxic layer.

Fins flaring, he caught the current and twisted upright. Hovering for a moment, fins stabilizing his aggressive descent, he paused before striking the seabed with the butt of the trident, sending a shower of blinding blue sparks cascading into the oppressive dark.

The light died in a bronze twinkle.

Swallowed whole.

For a moment, there was nothing.

Silence.

And then...

The current lifted in foggy interest, deepest shadows curling and writhing awake in a sluggish, groggy pull. And there, at the edges of his awareness, the whisper of ancient life drawn to the flash of light.

He smiled, showing teeth.

Not so barren after all.

Just... waiting.

For a king.

Planting his hand against the basalt wall, he fought the burn in the heavy water. The hostile edge of a place that was never made to accept a ruler.

But he was *Abyssari-born*. Bred for the weight and cold of the deep long before his people had been contained there. His scales were thicker than the other *Pelagorn* species—his bones heavy and dense enough for depths few others could endure.

His spines flicked, wicked and deadly. Holding posture in the beating heart of the trench. In any other sea, it was a lure for the drifting scavengers of the abyss.

Predators that couldn't endure here.

Not yet.

Still, he needed to be sure.

Thrumming low in his chest, he issued a summons.

It was a guttural hum, at first. Something beyond hearing, for it drummed in his chest. Using the dwindling oxygen reserved in his lungs, he made the water shimmer and the silt dance.

The Resonance.

A sub-audible purr.

In a rolling wave, his scales lifted. Venting heat from his coiled bulk.

And then he pulsed.

An intoxicating blue radiated from beneath his skin—the only shade of color the eyes of the deep could perceive in the anoxic dark.

Bioluminescence.

Symbiotic bacteria that nested in the grooves between his armored scales, bred in the dark, cultivated and fed on his heat. Agitated at his command.

It was the first of many specialized adaptations that set the *Abyssari* apart. Where his kind suffered in the open waters the *Thalassari* ruled, made vulnerable to disease in the warmth of rich shallows, the trench-born bloomed in the dark.

For a moment, the shadows retreated, recoiling from the new king twisting in the gloom, but that was all.

It was exactly as devoid of life as his father had always insisted.

A hollow court, waiting to be filled.

Pleased, he flicked his tail and shot through the ceiling of poison, and burst into a slightly less toxic layer. Pulling a few heaving breaths of burning brine over his gills, he floated in the seething dark.

Alone.

An abomination.

Exile.

The faces of his people flashed through his mind as he recovered his breath. Their disgust at his attempt to save them from extinction by crafting a siren from human flesh. And for his crimes—for mixing blood with a human—he'd been banished.

The verdict still echoed in his ears, as if they had not once done the same. As if, long before his birth, the *Abyssari* kings hadn't bred Sirens from mortal flesh. It was a truth recorded in their bloodlines, sung into the marrow of every human consort who'd once kept the seas docile for sailors in exchange for safe passage.

Fools.

Without the Sirens, the *Pelagorn* reign would have suffered and died out long ago.

But now they shrieked of blasphemy and corruption. They'd wrapped his failure around his gills and dragged him to the edge of his father's dwindling kingdom and cast him out.

Because he'd been careless.

Failed.

He'd chosen a human bride. Moved her toward a glorious conclusion that might've seen them escape the crushing authority of the *Thalassari* rule, and save his people from the brink.

But she'd died.

Drowned before he could set his knot, for he'd been too eager. Impatient. Overcome with the primal urge to breed, she'd been called to the sea before her rebirth had been complete.

It was a stain he'd carry in his marrow until redemption or death.

Lip curling, he flashed his teeth to the gloom.

He should let them choke, and the shallow king with them.

Filling his lungs with the burn, he returned to the void.

Because he had a new bride.

One he'd shape for this poisoned tide.

And from her womb, he would spawn a new breed of *Pelagorn.* One equal to the harshest conditions known to any of the seas.

He would not fail again.

This time, he would take his time. Obsess over every possible precaution and shape her pathetic, fragile body into something truly divine, no matter the cost to himself.

The trench pressed at him from every angle until his bones ached and his muscles strained against the weight.

Lips pulling into a vicious grin, he swept through the trench.

Let those dying fools reject him. This hollow pit, this crushing abyss would incubate his kingdom.

And she would crown it.

Tail lashing, he broke the currents and disturbed the silt, blending the layers of poisonous water for the first time in eons.

Chest aching with the sour burn, he cut through the gloom and unclipped the pouch lashed to his waist. Fingers working the knot until it came loose, and the polyps inside churned. Fed their first taste of the waters that would become their home.

The Raskoril.

A parasitic strain of coral, engineered to thrive in the choking cold. Meant to thrive without sunlight or warm, fertile currents.

This species was bred for the trench.

Colonized from parasites and fed from the veins of the last *Abyssari* king.

He'd stolen it. Cultivated the larva, starved the polyps of sunlight, and now? He'd feed the colony a steady diet of venom and blood.

Corrupting it. Coaxing it into something new. Until every outcropping of the budding colony bore his mark.

It was to be the seeds of his kingdom. The roots of his reef, upon which he would craft an empire enslaved to him alone.

Dipping his claws, he began the arduous task ahead and went to work. Seeding the trench.

Preparing the seabed, he used the trident to raise the tide, to wash away the silt cloaking the seabed in aeons of sediment.

With a snap of his tail, he drove upward once more, scattering the polyps into the open throat of the trench. Letting them drift in the wake of his passing, where they would settle against the seabed. Setting little anchors that would pierce deep into the basalt, filtering the fetid waters one tiny breath at a time.

And thus, the Raskoril Coral would oxygenate the deep.

His hand plunged into the pouch, again and again, each fling of his wrist cast a net that would bind the primitive shadows and allow life to breathe here, where no other had been able to endure.

With each pass, the water grew thicker. Pulsing with a slow hum as they set down roots, their glow fanning across sheer rock walls.

A reef, born in exile.

One that would endure. Grow where he commanded, and feast directly from his veins. Nurse at his spines and fill their tiny bellies with venom.

He could sense it already—the looming specter of a ghostly structure, a skeleton of what would rise. A cradle for his bride, it would house their brood when her body no longer belonged to the surface.

The thought was invasive. An urge he hadn't expected, but one that dragged a snarl from his chest and sent him back through the layers as the first threads of blue shimmered across the basalt.

Gills flaring, his chest expanded, lungs filling with the poisoned current.

It wasn't enough.

Elegant limbs flashed in his mind. Shattered bone wrapped in fragile flesh.

Heat coiled in muscles starved of oxygen, forcing him to ascend. Unable to resist the carnal pull he felt to return to the surface.

And now, there was time to indulge, for the trench had been sown. Tender roots threaded through the darkness needed time to incubate and spread.

Time he would use to initiate his bride with another dose. Feed her careful, measured sips of venom, a little at a time, even as he obliterated her womb and prepared her for what *he* needed. Pumping her full of sperm until she was ready to take all of him.

All without repeating the mistakes of the past.

Denying himself the ecstasy of truly claiming her, for he would never be able to truly breed a human.

No, the knot at the base of his cock was meant to secure a mate, to hold his chosen female in place as they drifted through the current for long hours. An anchor set in place meant as a water-tight seal that would allow his seed to move deep enough that the sea could not simply wash it away.

No, he couldn't breed a human.

But a Siren?

A Siren was meant to take all of him.

It would be a delicate balance. One slip, one moment of hazy control, and he would ruin her.

Propelling himself forward, the exiled prince left the fledgling reef behind. The waters grew warmer as he swam through the layers of this poisoned chalice. And his gills flushed vibrant red as he ascended too fast, blood fizzing with tiny, agonizing bubbles as he struggled to draw a single breath not laced with brutal acid.

Breaking through the ceiling of that final lethal layer, he emerged into the shallows and drew water over his gills that sent relief immediately bleeding through his system.

Reeling from the punishment, he paused in the rich, warm water until the ache subsided.

But the pain had only sharpened his resolve.

Reminded him of what was at stake.

Even now, he could smell her. His bride. Both foreign and intoxicating, hers was a scent that called to him to do heinous, wicked things. Vile acts that would have risked banishment from his father's court.

But of course...

He was alone.

Unbound by the laws of the open-water king who'd condemned the trench-born to a long, slow death. Unmoored, he'd been freed from the judgment of those who'd rather wither in obscurity than fight the *Thalassari* king.

There was none who might block him.

Not a soul who could stop what he would unleash upon that dainty, fragile female marooned in the middle of an uninhabited ocean.

Here, in the Black Sea, Nyxarion Korrides was the law.

And he would have his bride, in whichever manner he chose.

Settling in the surf, still partially submerged, he allowed himself to pause. Recuperate. Flushing the brine from his gills, he blocked the only exit.

And smiled.

It was almost time to begin.

CHAPTER 6

*O*ne cheek soaking in a shallow tidal pool, her lips caressed by the salt of this unknown sea, Kore whined. A keening moan of pain that broke through the dregs of fitful sleep. Anguish that radiated out from a broken heart, only to throb in a shattered body.

Bruises bloomed across pale, water-logged flesh. Trauma so violent, it had left her legs speckled in a mosaic of molted black and green. Etched with shades of vibrant purple and speckled with a sickly shade of yellow.

Evidence of what she'd endured at the bottom of the Aegean Sea. The damage that should have been enough to end her, but wasn't.

Groaning, Kore turned her back to the sun.

Hiding her face from Apollo's blistering gaze—it was an unconscious action, but one that held significant weight nevertheless, for even in her delirium, she turned away from her lord.

Water dripped from the ceiling above. Splashing across her brow. Lapping at her cheek with gentle, insistent waves.

Kore flinched, jerked from a dream of glittering scales and sheets of impossible, undulating muscle, she sucked a breath between chapped, dehydrated lips. Spluttering as she worked to peel her lids apart.

He'd returned.

Lying just there.

Sleeping on his side, half in, half out of the water. The tide was high. Water lapping at the mouth of the cave, enabling him to block the only exit with a body she couldn't make sense of.

A body straight from the annals of myth.

Blinking in the gloom, Kore stole the chance to *really* look. Scarcely daring to breathe, she inspected the impossibly broad expanse of his back, where dense muscle became elegant scale and man became leviathan.

Wicked spines were laid flat, almost flush against his scales. Harmless in their net of gossamer webbing, dozens of fins were tucked tight to his tail. It was a limb more than three times thicker than she was wide, the first mighty fluke rocked above the surface in time with the pulse of each gentle wave, while the second was submerged in dark waters. Peaking above the surface, it flicked with an unconscious grace that begged to be returned to the sea.

In slumber, his breath was rattling and heavy, but as steady as the ocean itself. In any other, that rattle would hold the ominous jangle of death.

But in a creature such as this?

She shivered.

A wave splashed against his scales.

He flinched.

Spines flicking high as his fins flared, it was an unconscious defense that sent Kore cringing back. Away. Clinging to the shadows at the back of her lonely, sodden cave. Terrified that he would wake and turn his attention upon her once more.

To what end, she did not know and couldn't begin to guess.

She stayed like that for countless, frantic beats of her heart. Unblinking. Her breath shallow as she waited to drown beneath the next crushing wave of despair the gods might send to test her faith.

And there she remained. Cowering in the dark. Knees drawn up and pressed to her chest. Sitting in a shallow pool of tide water warmed not by the sun, but by the heat of her body. Unmoving until it occurred to her that she should not be alive enough to know fear. Not warm enough to heat water. That she should have died with the other priestesses, if not by drowning, then crushed to nothing beneath the weight of a broken ship grinding her into the sea floor.

Her pelvis had been crushed.

Her legs pulverized beneath the weight of a ruined slave ship.

But she was… whole.

Frowning, Kore looked past her knee. Inspecting the mottled colors blooming beneath her once-golden, sun-kissed skin. She flexed her toes, noting the sluggish response from the digits on her left foot. The swollen, disfigured contusion jutting out just beneath her right kneecap.

An injury that should have been crippling, but wasn't.

Ugly though it was, she could scarcely feel the pain.

Clouds shaded the sun's ferocity, sending shadows to dance across the foamy peaks lapping at the cave entrance and the creature blocking her exit.

And then she noticed it.

The glow.

A spiderweb of eerie blue lines pulsed beneath her skin. Delicate as spider's silk, it was the exact shade of lightning when Zeus' temper flared—and just as shocking for it should not exist beneath her skin!

Veins filled with something more than a commoner's blood, she had been infused with something… else.

Swallowing, her throat ravaged and dry, Kore tore her eyes away from the disturbing sight. Choking back the nausea, she moved. Stealing forward on legs impossibly free of pain. Placing one trembling hand on slick moss, she pulled herself forward, inch by silent, quaking inch.

Crawling across the slime exposed by the retreating tide, skating around the tiny things that thrived in tidal pools, she timed her every breath with the crash of the next wave. Approaching Poseidon's son until she was close enough to see his scales shift with each rattling, disturbing breath.

Fingers twisting, she paused long enough to call on her Lord. Silently begging Apollo to intervene. To deliver her from this lonely spit of forgotten land.

The sun only sank deeper behind the clouds.

A rattling breath snared Kore's attention, and she looked. Eyes catching on the flutter and stretch of that peculiar sound.

Gills.

It was the rattle of gills clapping together as the beast worked to draw breath outside of his natural element.

Sweat dappled Kore's nape.

For she knew.

There was only one way off this island.

And this, her only chance to do something. To try, no matter how futile the hope that she could win. That she might outswim a son of Poseidon and find freedom, claim the chance to return to her homeland, and help them rebuild the temple of Delphi with the intimate knowledge of the divine she now clearly possessed.

Crouching low, she took careful, timed steps toward the beast. Aiming to slip between the fluke of his tail and the cave wall, she toiled. Back aching. Legs trembling. Her every breath hissing between lips pressed thin and bloodless.

Only when she was close enough to touch did she dare to tear her eyes from his grotesque form and sight her exit.

Three steps.

Just three careful, diligent steps, and she could slip into the waves of this unknown sea and swim. To where, she didn't know and couldn't bring herself to care.

There was only the hope that this could be the beginning of her freedom. An end to the series of events that had landed her here.

Setting one dainty, bruised foot atop a flattened stone, Kore shifted her weight forward. Careful not to lend too much to the movement until she was certain the footing would not betray her.

Success made her dizzy, and she let go a silent, trembling breath as she balanced between the next step and a fate she couldn't begin to comprehend.

Reaching for a handhold, she found an anchor in the stone and moved to claim her next step.

It happened in a blur.

A misplaced hand.

A rock gull, nesting where she couldn't see.

And a gust of wind that seemed to mock her, by dispelling the cloud cover in a brilliant, blinding instant.

With a honking cry, the gull took flight.

Composure shattering, Kore gasped and staggered back.

And the creature jolted.

Spines flaring, he reacted. Instinctual. Primal. Impaling Kore when she tried to scramble for purchase and found herself clawing at empty air until her feet were beneath her once more.

Crying out, her hands went to the spine embedded in her thigh, and she pulled. Wrenching herself free with a sob, she scrambled back from iridescent scales. Back from the flex and twist of an impossible body. Away from the leviathan as he woke, and luminous, alien eyes scoured the dark in search of his prey.

Her lips parted on a scream that was murdered before it had even been born.

In its place, liquid fire gushed through her veins.

Gasping, she looked and found the wound. A gaping, inky

hole leaking sluggish blood tainted black. Big enough to fit three fingers inside—with dark, ominous veins spidering out.

Venom.

Horrified, she watched the toxin move. Spreading with each frantic, terrified beat of her heart, it pulsed as it surged through her veins and made her skin bulge.

Sobbing now, Kore turned to flee. To retreat into the dank, dark little cave and its harmless puddles of misery.

And in so doing…

… exposed her back to a predator…

CHAPTER 7

*M*olten heat surged through Kore's veins. Alien arousal that spread as her heart flailed and thrashed, each fluttering lurch a treachery that pumped the venom deeper. Faster. Swamping her with the sort of liquid inferno that drew a choked gasp from her lips. Forced her fingers to curl into hooked claws as she tried to drag herself away. To claim some fragile, doomed whisper of safety.

But her body betrayed her.

Limbs that had been broken and miraculously healed no longer obeyed her whims. Knees that had been bent in supplication to a sun god were now scraped and stained with algae, damp with the lingering breath of the ocean—stained by the shifting, treacherous shadows lurking beneath the waves.

Quaking, her muscles heavy with feverish heat, Kore tried to fight the slick stone. Tried to scramble and scrape as she fled the beast who was inside her, now.

In her blood.

Throttled by a gasp, she choked on a sob as her muscles quaked. Heavy and languid, she grew clumsy as the toxin spread.

Her movements sloppy even as her fingertips tore against the rocks. Skin rubbed ragged and raw went unnoticed.

But her thigh?

It throbbed.

Tugging at her sanity.

Leaking thick, sluggish blood, dark veins spidered out from the tear in her flesh. Drawing every spare ounce of her attention as the wound flushed hot and ominous.

A sound crackled through her lips. Thin with terror, it was a fragile thing. Pathetic. Flailing, her heart lurched in her chest, crashing against her ribs as Kore clawed for distance. Trying to claim the foolish hope that she might escape this fate. This horrible prison with its impossible, mythic guard.

It wasn't the pain.

It wasn't the fear of what might become of her—she was far too traumatized for all that.

No, it was the inferno unfurling within her.

Dark.

Vile.

Insidious. It was the sort of heat that pooled low in her belly. Drawing a gush of slick moisture from deep inside, her breath hitched when she felt her heartbeat drop low. Pulsing in a place that only her Lord Apollo and his consecrated priests were meant to know.

Arousal flushed in her cheeks. An alien glow that grew more visceral with every passing moment. Cresting toward something heinous with each panting, shallow breath that splattered past her lips.

"Nooo," she moaned and squeezed her eyes shut. Teeth sinking into the inside of her cheek. Hard enough to taste the coppery tang of her own blood.

Such was her futile attempt to resist.

It did nothing to banish the fever—if anything, her refusal only drove the obscene sensitivity humming in her skin higher.

Nipples peaked beneath the tattered remnants of her robe, Kore's breath grew haggard as the rough-spun fabric tormented those delicate peaks. Chafing with each tiny movement, a bolt rippled through her sinew and landed in the hollow between her legs.

It struck with the force of a gong.

Horror tightened her throat.

A sick, twisted humiliation that blended with the toxin's wrath. Demanding. Unrelenting as it pounded through her.

And then she heard it.

Something other than the desperate, rattling breaths she dragged through her lips.

A whisper that was more than the roar of blood rushing in her ears, or the quiet pulsing slap of water on stone.

At first, it was scarcely more than a low rumble. Subaudible. A thing felt in her bones and jelly.

But the answer was a gush of molten interest.

Haggard breath escaped her throat on the heels of a guttural moan. And she turned. Tried to hide what was obvious inside a lie dressed in horrified truth.

Her terror.

Her revulsion.

It was a pale wisp in the shadow of what pulsed between her legs.

Dragging herself backward, palms scrambling for purchase on slippery stone, Kore pressed back. Deeper. Her nails splintering and cracking as she forced her body to obey. To flee. Scuttling into the darkest recesses of that lonely cave, where the shadows were deep enough to swallow her whole.

It was a hole with no exit.

A pit where terrified, primitive things went to hide from death.

Where she fought to be.

As if summoned, movement from the shallows echoed all

around her. The glimmer of iridescent scales skittered across the ceiling, reflecting the last rays of the sun in a mocking flash that should have been feminine and dainty but… wasn't.

Scales rasped over stone. Wet. Sinister, crunching movement. It was menace in motion. Sinuous and serpentine, even where she couldn't see it.

She caught a glimpse of flared spines.

The surging bulge of alien muscle as a dense coil rose, then fell. Undulating closer.

She blinked away the salty burn of unnoticed tears. Frozen as she watched. Waited.

And a shadow filled the window of sunlight.

Male. Utterly so, despite their profound differences. It was obvious in the harsh lines of heavily muscled shoulders. The rippling shadows cascading down over his chest. Racing toward the line between man and Leviathan. Where skin met scales.

Her breath caught, high at the back of her throat, her every instinct screaming to flee—but she was pinned to the back of that cave.

Eyes.

Dark and fathomless. Gleaming in the low light.

Summoning the last of her will, she pushed herself back and managed to claim a handspan more before the venom wrenched a low, breathless moan from her lips. Cheeks scalded with mortified heat, she watched as a ripple passed through his body. Morbidly fascinated by the gills that flared with a slow, deliberate inhale.

Nostrils growing pinched and white at the edges, he sucked a breath between his lips.

Breathing her in.

Exhaling an unspoken, hissing command that rolled through her bones, his lips pulled taut in a grimace. Vibrating in her chest, her organs… and her weeping, treacherous core.

Molten heat gushed between her legs, soaking her thighs.

Pooling on the stone beneath her, she wetted tattered robes in a rush of shameful arousal she couldn't fight. The wound in her thigh all but forgotten.

"Please," she whispered, "I don't—I can't—"

She was sodden.

Ashamed.

Feet slipping in the wet, she squirmed. Thighs gliding where she was slick and oozing, her flesh swollen. Ripe. Agitating what was meant to be chaste.

What had been promised to her Lord Apollo, before it had been desecrated by a slave trader and now… poisoned by a beast.

Horrified, she squealed and felt that heat curl low. Pooling between her hips. Twisting with a power she couldn't begin to fathom.

A wet, rasping breath spattered over the beast's lips…

… and a cord was plucked. Tied to her ichor, that sound strummed at something deep and primal. Something woven through muscle and marrow. A hooked barb that dragged a sob from her chest, even as it brought forth another creamy gush.

At first, the beast was still, but for the unsettling flap of gills flexing below his jaw.

And then… his lips twitched.

A smile stretched over gleaming, pearlescent teeth in exactly the right way to keep her pinned in place. Stuck.

It was a horrible thing, his smile.

Because it was… hungry.

Ravenous.

His gills rippled on a cough.

And with a huff, he lifted the heavy coil of his tail and twisted deeper into the cave. Snaking closer. Every movement serpentine. Alien. So utterly foreign, Kore couldn't so much as draw breath as he surged forward with a methodical grace that was at once repulsive and hypnotic.

At his approach, her heart thrashed. A pathetic flail that

pushed the venom into every secret, forbidden part of her. All the hidden corners that had been promised to the glory of Apollo's gaze were corrupted by something… desperate.

Something wanton and wicked, for it was no longer a mere flutter in her throat, but a deep, rhythmic throb centered between her trembling thighs.

A whimper escaped her, then. Eyes wide, dread flushed hot in cheeks stained red with mortified heat. "Please," she rasped again. A quiet, desperate plea—not to the beast, but to the Lord she'd forsaken. "Please, please save me."

Kore twisted her fingers in a mockery of Apollo's sacred symbol. A stumbling, broken version of the prayer she'd offered since she'd been given to the temple. It was a trembling, desperate invocation against the monster looming before her. Pitiful. A thing already half forgotten.

A laugh echoed between them, making her ribs tremble. Cruel and low. It was a ripple of sound that skated over her skin like a whip, but landed with the crashing weight of the sea.

Inhuman.

He inched closer, heat radiating from scaled flesh she could feel even in the cold depths of her chosen prison. But it wasn't the cruel gleam, nor the sinister intent glimmering in his alien glare.

It was the angry thing jutting up from below his belly button.

A cock.

She'd heard the word grunted through browning teeth in the slave market. Heard it hissed above her as a man who'd paid to own her had helped himself to what had always been saved to honor Apollo.

But this was no tender spear of human flesh.

Her gaze was fixed to a thing that defied all reason.

It was to be her doom.

All she saw was a glimpse. A hint between one instant and the next.

It was enough.

Enough that she squealed, pressing back hard enough to bruise her spine even as her core gushed and fluid oozed from deep inside.

And so it was that the same word surfaced in her mind as she looked at the hideous thing moving toward her. Monstrous. A cock of truly demonic proportions, it would have shamed the Athenian slavers and made the priests of Delphi fall to their knees in shocked worship of the divine.

A glistening bead burped from the tip before it was swallowed by shadows.

And with a lash of his tail, he was upon her.

His clawed hand caught her throat. Lifting her as if she weighed nothing at all, he brought her up, level with his eyes. Air strangled in her chest, her legs kicking uselessly as he studied her.

Amused.

He was *amused* by her horror.

Aroused by it.

With a growl of mockery, the beast tore through the flimsy robes growing tattered and wretched, baring fevered flesh to that slitted, mocking glare. Inspecting, he let one hand trail south, claws bumping over nipples and ribs, rimming her belly button before he dipped… lower.

The threat of claws touched her swollen heat and came away wet.

He showed her. Spreading two fingers in a lewd 'V' so she could see the strings of sticky drool spreading between his digits. They glinted in the gloom. Tacky. Mocking her.

His grin grew feral.

Gills clattering.

Cruel madness flashed in his eyes.

And then he tasted her.

Obscene. Lingering.

Sucking those fingers, he let his tongue sweep between them and watched her writhe without so much as a tepid blink. Drinking her in as he swallowed her down.

Strangling where she was held aloft, back pinned to the cave wall, Kore flailed. Struggling to draw breath, even as a dam broke and a flood of obscene wetness gushed between her legs, she watched as he tasted her. Disgusted.

Enthralled.

She couldn't help the sound she made as she stared. A desperate, animal whine.

The beast was far from finished, yet unhurried.

There was nothing but time to enjoy his hooked minnow.

Something wicked flicked across his face, then. Something… devious and hungry.

Lifting her higher still, his fingers flexed where they were wrapped about her throat. With the other, he tore at what little remained of her robes, stripping her bare to a gaze ill-suited for the semi-dark of the cave.

A gaze meant for the Deep.

His gills clapped, as a wet, sucking breath rattled between them.

And then, catching her left knee and wrenching her thighs apart, his head dipped…

… so he could drink from the source.

Hot and slick, a possessive swipe of his tongue lapped at folds sopping with shame. Drenched in terrorized humiliation. Saturated in a treacherous betrayal of everything she'd sworn to be.

Pleasure ignited her blood, and she sobbed through the vice circling her throat.

He denied her even that. Flexing cruel digits, he crushed that sound against his palm and left her dangling from his grip.

Helpless.

Desecrated as the feast began.

His tongue darted out. Slipping between plumped folds.

Dividing sacred petals, he sucked her back and swallowed her down. Making a mess of her. Lewd in the way he pulled at her lips and made her plump.

Blackness yawned at her peripherals, but Kore arched into that obscene touch. Hips tilting of their own accord, she stretched toward what promised to unbalance her entire world.

Biting at exposed skin, he feasted. The air frigid against heated flesh.

Fed by terror, Kore grew bold. And scrambling hands found purchase against forearms corded with dense muscle. Trying to pry him away from her airway. Trying to protect, even as he lapped and sucked.

She made a sound, then.

A pathetic, desperate croon that rattled in the palm of his hand when his tongue snaked deeper. Probing inside her. Penetrating that tight sheath, he made her clench on a gasp when teeth scraped at sensitive, overwrought flesh.

She couldn't breathe. Couldn't think.

Couldn't fight or move or beg.

There was nothing beyond the pressure of something building.

Something terrible and impossible.

And then she felt him smile.

Lips pressed against sodden folds. Twitching with mirth, cruel. She knew without seeing it… that it was a gesture meant to taunt.

Tears spilled over her lashes, then. Hot and wretched. Scalding burning cheeks as she sobbed in the heart of his palm and looked toward the rocky ceiling above.

But Apollo could not see her.

Not here. Where she'd been trapped in the dark by a monster.

Going limp, even as her centre tightened with wanton treachery, Kore willed her end to be swift. Ignoring the way her thighs were pried further apart, so he might dig yet further inside, she felt her belly grow taut. Reacting to a beast, she gushed where shame pooled between her legs. Where she was soggy and swollen.

Aching.

The son of Poseidon built a fire in the middle of a nameless ocean.

Fanning the flames with a sweep of his tongue, he pushed her into the inferno, grinning now as her spine bowed and she pressed deeper into that wriggling, wet warmth, and then—

Peeling himself away, the beast thumbed the river of glistening cream as it ran down his chin.

Gills fluttering, he sucked his digits clean…

… and let her fall.

She landed in a heap of trembling, twisted limbs and clenching flesh.

Discarded.

Left to cower as he rose to his full height and balanced on a fat coil of sinuous tail.

And then he reached for the monstrous thing pulsing below his navel. Stroked it.

It was an action she'd seen the priest of Apollo do, tugging on his wrinkled little cock with white knuckles as sweat dropped from his temples and spattered across Kore's belly.

It was a thing the man at the slave market had done, too, as cruel greed gleamed in his yellowed, watery eyes and he spurted ropes of fetid cream in the dirt at her feet.

But this?

She had no words to describe *this*.

The beast's hand was large enough to crush her ribs, and still, his cock looked enormous in that clawed grip.

And then it… *moved*. Belching up a gush of shimmering brine, the thing flexed when it was petted, as if preening for attention. As if eager for a task.

Agast, Kore watched as it tried to buck its master's grip and reached instead... for her.

Undulating, an eerie mockery of something sentient, it strained against the cage of thick fingers. Surging in size and shrinking from one instant to the next. Pulsing a grotesque dance of the obscene.

She went limp beneath his palm, growing weak as the fight spluttered at her edges. Starved of breath, but still, she couldn't look away. Couldn't tear her gaze from what he fisted in one hand.

Lips tingling, eyes bulging as her pulse pounded in her jelly, something taboo clawed its way free of her chest. "Please..."

Her knees hit the stone in a wet clatter.

Gasping, she gulped down a breath of air. Head lolling as her tiny, horrific world spun around her.

She blinked, dazed.

Shocked and helpless, she mustered a tiny, wordless protest as she was flipped to her hands and knees. Palms scraped raw when she slapped the rock in a pathetic attempt to flee.

But her thighs were wrenched wide. The air at her back heavy with menace, even as a chill kissed her sopping flesh.

A rough palm landed between her shoulder blades, grinding her flat to the stone. Her cheek mashed against the cold surface as she was pried apart. Left open to inspection or... worse.

The beast captured her hips. Tilting her up and open, he took liberties. Probing delicate folds with vicious claws.

She was ruined. Desperate. Slick and twitching even under such crude handling, he wound her tighter with every careful sweep of those deadly digits. The threat of violence prickled between her legs, and she mewled. Betrayed by her own flesh.

And then she felt it.

Wet.

Alive.

Tentative, at first.

Inquisitive.

It slithered against her mound. Thick and blunt. Unnaturally hot. Greasier than her slit, but so utterly, horribly alive with intent.

Her body knew what her mind rejected.

Hips tilting as if bound to a breeding bench, a dam awaiting a stud, her knees pressed wider still.

That compliance was rewarded. Probing wetness traced her folds. Rimming that clenching slit with deliberate precision, before it moved… higher. Throbbing against a swollen bead of pleasure, it pumped between her lips. Teasing. Wretched.

Divine.

Kore bucked in terror. Muscles flinching in horrified protest as that weapon curled and flexed against her. Leaving the beast to savor every pathetic shudder he might draw from her frame.

Pinned beneath him, her mind pushed to the edge of breaking, she could only sob as he explored her with slow, invasive cruelty—touching every inch. Marking every secret place Kore had ever cherished.

And all the while, her body throbbed.

Open.

Dripping…

… *Ready.*

CHAPTER 8

Cruel hands pinned her to unyielding stone, forcing an inelegant grunt to burp from Kore's lips. Dazed, she squirmed. Slick and trembling. Arms laid out to either side, she was stretched. Exposed. Vulnerable to the deadly whisper of claws as they raked over her skin.

Gooseflesh erupted across her every exposed inch, and she gasped when he dragged the swollen folds of her pussy apart. Peeling her open. Wide enough that even the cold air was a violation.

It was deliberate.

A slow, methodical torment.

An… *inspection.*

Of everything that would soon belong to him.

She knew it.

Remembered just the way she'd been investigated in the slave market. Like chattel. Like she wasn't a holy woman sworn to the very deity whose merciless heat had left her shoulders flaking and her lips chapped as the unwashed masses looked on.

But now?

With an inhuman weight pressing her to damp, slick stone?

Her shame burned hotter than anything else she'd ever known—hotter still when she felt the first glide of something blunt.

His... cock.

It was monstrous.

Slick with its own lubrication, she felt it slither between her folds. Snaking through all that was soaking and gooey with obscene ease.

Kore could only whimper, the tiny sound swallowed up by the rasp of scales on stone, heavy breaths, and the *schlick-flap* of gills clapping above her in the gloom.

Shifting, he collected both of her wrists in a sweep of one massive hand, then dragged her arms in front of her face. Stretching her out as if the flex of her protests meant nothing.

Knuckles rolled down her spine, then. Tumbling over vertebrae, her ribs, until his palm found an anchor on her lower back. Braced on one hand, keeping her wrists pinned, his muscles quivering with scarcely contained restraint, he balanced on one hand and tilted her hips up. Open.

Leaving no inch of her untouched.

That living weight curled back.

Seeking...

... *entrance.*

Breath catching, Kore thrashed. "No—"

It burrowed.

Claws dimpled her hip.

It burrowed.

The stretch was unbearable. A cruel test of her limits. A trial meant to be endured by birthing mothers, not... not drowned holy women forgotten in the dark.

Still.

A wet, sucking breath flapped above her, and his cock flexed against her entrance. Too wide. Pulsing with unholy insistence.

Burrowing.

Kore's entire world grew narrow and refined. Reduced to a single point, she went still. Utterly fixated on that relentless pressure as the monster's weight at her back increased.

He was refused entry. Her gates resisted what wasn't meant to be. No matter the ache, nor the slick fluid pouring from her depths, she kept what he meant to take.

Scales rasped against stone as he shifted with a grunt. A rattling breath. He repositioned. Touch brimming with violence, he slowed. Withdrew.

Then, setting the full weight of his colossal body against the basin of upturned, female hips, he forced submission.

Pain.

It lanced through her.

A bright, searing thing that made her sob against stone. Just for an instant. A flame so bright, she couldn't help but lean toward the heat before she was swallowed by shadow.

Shamed.

He *burrowed.*

Worming inside, he churned against her with relentless pulses. Stretching what had been given to Apollo, she was ruined. Defiled and reshaped to fit the king of monsters.

He made a sound. Something other than the wet rattle of death, it was a thing almost beyond hearing. A rumble that shivered through her marrow and echoed between her thighs.

She couldn't help it, the way she clenched. Bearing down.

Fingers twisting where they were pinned beneath his fist, she tried to call upon her Lord. Even as she gushed for a beast, she tried. To resist. To reject. Railing against every brutal inch that was stolen. Remade.

A futile thing.

Heat pooled in her belly. Grew damp and flush as sweat speckled her brow. Pooling in the dip at her lower back, where scales met flesh.

And her pussy. It spasmed.

Milking that repulsive thing as it burrowed, *burrowed, burrowed.*

Robbing her of sense.

It was her turn to gasp, and she did it through a flood of salty tears. Shaking. Trembling.

And then... he stopped.

Cock throbbing where it had wrenched her open, he pinned her flat to the stone. Holding her still, as if to let her grow accustomed to the stretch, he raked deadly claws down her ribs. Bumping over bone as she lay gasping beneath him.

He was... petting her. Almost... soothing.

But that was impossible. *He was inside her.* Brutally. Fully. Seated so deep, her lungs strained for space to fill.

Still, the pacifying flick of a somewhat gentle touch continued to trace flushed skin.

Time ceased. The trickle of seconds replaced with shivering breaths.

She was left to do nothing but feel.

Every inch.

Each pounding beat of his enormous heart.

Penetrated.

Remade.

There was nothing. *She* was nothing.

There was only the suffocating weight, the maddening throb, and a stretch that grew less alien, less unbearable with every passing instant.

And yet he remained. Balanced on one hand, a living tentacle buried inside her. Motionless, as if waiting.

Slick dripped from where she gaped, a drop of pure shame wetting the stone. She felt it slip from her mound. Oozing from petals stretched white and bloodless.

Kore gasped. Fluttering as her walls hugged a beast.

Another low rumble shook her marrow, then.

Approval.

She could feel it hanging heavy in the damp air.

And without warning, he moved. Relenting. Scales scraping delicate flesh, he ground against her. Ravaging her thighs with the slightest movement, each cruel, deliberate circle of his hips forced a ragged groan from her throat.

She was pried open with merciless precision.

At her back, the weight of a Leviathan. And with his free hand, he wound a fist into her salt-matted hair and wrenched her head back. Making her arch as she was laid open. All but folded in half.

Something pathetic escaped her, then. A whimper bred with a grunt. Some disgraceful call of a broken thing being fucked in the dark.

Desperate to throw him off, to preserve some scrap of the dignity she'd been meant to wear, she snarled. Writhing beneath him.

It was a terrible mistake.

It only drove him deeper. Jerking hips an invite she hadn't meant to issue, but couldn't rescind.

Fist growing tight and cruel against her scalp, he growled low. Breath wet. Forcing her spine to bow as he gave yet more of his weight.

And his cock… it bulged inside her. Growing impossibly fat. Each lazy churn of turgid flesh was a punishment that made her sob. Broken.

Betrayed.

For her clit…

It had become… engorged. Fat and swollen, it, more than any other terrible thing in that dank little cave, had become the center of her world. Desperate. Throbbing with unnatural need. It forced out all rational thought and screamed for *more.*

She pushed back. Seeking friction.

A brainless beast in unnatural heat, Kore tried to answer that primal call being written into her flesh. Sobbing, her knees spread of their own accord, and she made room for it—her destruction. An invitation scrawled in gooey slime and flushed cheeks.

Betrayal lit her every nerve.

What little remained of her mind rejected the horror being inflicted upon the body.

Still.

Her hips shunted back in shameless need.

Gills rattled above her with another grotesque *schlick-flap.*

And then, without warning, he withdrew. Pausing at her entrance. Making her hiss.

At the loss.

The stretch.

A shattered whine spattered over her lips. It was a plea.

The sound above her—behind her—was smug, in its damp clatter. She knew without looking that full lips were stretched over a grin.

And then she knew nothing else.

Bullying his way back inside, he filled her in a slow, crushing grind that had her clawing at stone, even as she pushed back and set her knees to take it.

Humiliation. Shame. Pain.

Everything faded. There was only…

… this.

The sharp, dizzying edge of pleasure. Forbidden, sickening ecstasy blossomed between her legs, despite the twist of her fingers or the whispers turning to ash on her tongue.

"Gods, *no,*" she groaned and choked on a sob.

He'd found her end. Stuffed her so full of cock she could taste the brine on the back of her tongue.

Something tacky and wet dripped down her thighs. A slow ooze that only wound her tighter.

And still he didn't fuck her.

At least, not in the sweaty, desperate way the slaver had, when he'd tested the product he'd bought. Not in the reverent way Apollo's priest had, when he'd tried to put a divine son between her legs.

This? It was… different.

As alien to the men she'd been with as his species was to hers.

Instead of pumping her full, he settled for filling her up. Grinding against her upturned bottom. Churning inside her.

Almost…

Almost as if he was training her.

And he was.

Stretching her open until her hole twitched around him, begging as that hideous thing inside her pulsed against her limit. Twisting and sucking.

Claws raked her spine in a caress both painful and gentle, before that grip found an anchor in her bedraggled locks.

Wrenching her head backward, he forced her chest flat and abandoned her wrists, only to turn her hips up. Adjusting the angle to suit his sinister design.

A wet grunt splashed above her, and she felt scales bunch against her ass. Rubbing her raw with a single push, he slithered back.

And crammed himself back inside.

Kore grunted as the air was forced from her lungs. "Hung-ghh." Torturing everything that was swollen and slick. Enough that her mind went flat and blank.

It was the friction—the lack. It stole her breath, robbed her spirit of the fire she needed to fight.

Shredded her mind and left her with nothing but need.

A low rumble sounded behind her.

Smug. Goading.

Each cruel, serpentine stroke made her spasm. Every withdrawal a torment she chased, as if she wasn't being dragged inside out. As if his cock alone *wasn't* enough to lift her body off the stone.

It started with a spasm.

Uncontrollable. Something vile that rose in the chasm between empty and brutally stuffed.

And then, muffled against unyielding rock and putrid moss, she whispered, "Please," in a voice she didn't recognize. "Please, I... I can't—I need—"

Thrumming low in his chest, he rewarded her with another heavy grind that plundered Apollo's sacred bounty. Claws dimpling her hip, his grip was enormous. Crushing. Possessive.

She bucked against that fist, using it. Hips working, she squirmed as slick gushed and squished from between her lips.

Breath hot against her nape, the grip in her hair grew tight. Cruel. Pinning her to the stone, he pumped her with careful, deliberate strokes. Holding her trembling body exactly where he wanted it.

"Gods," she rasped between thrusts, eyes unseeing. Lips gaping. "Please! Stop... I don't understand..."

There was pressure building where she was sodden. Something forbidden and... incredible.

Pleasure.

It pulsed hot and violent in her blood. In the hole he'd ruined and remade to suit himself.

Her world shattered as that impossible pleasure ripped through her. Spasming, she lurched where she was hooked. Flailing as much as she might, her shame gushed from her depths in torrents. Slick soaking his cock as she convulsed.

Openly weeping, pinned and broken beneath him, she gave everything that had been meant for Apollo.

Another rumble shook her marrow, then. A low, predatory

sound of savage satisfaction—it could be mistaken for nothing else.

Crooning against her nape, she shuddered when he pressed a grin to her cheek.

And pumped back inside.

She knew, then.

He hadn't even begun.

CHAPTER 9

Broken open on a cock not meant for mortals, Kore was impaled. Face down against damp rock in the back of a grim, dank little cave. Breathless. Her hips caught in a punishing grip. Tilted to suit the whims of a monster.

Stretched beyond what she'd ever thought possible around a spear of flesh that had ruined her.

Utterly.

Pinned with careful, vicious claws that prickled with every twitch from her abused, gaping pussy. The beast had gone still, seeming to enjoy each flutter of climax still rippling through her overwrought body. Kneading the meat of her hip as if in reward for milking his shaft, the point of deadly claws a subtle demand for compliance. A threat, as if she might succeed in wriggling free. As if the weight of a leviathan wasn't slung across her back.

As if she wasn't impaled so deep she could taste the brine.

And his cock.

It… squirmed within her, triggering another gush of fluid. Another flutter of muscles rippling along that foreign girth that had no business fitting inside her fragile human walls.

Pumping her of its own accord, it moved. Separate from its

master. Stroking her deep in something that would be easy to mistake for a caress, but wasn't.

It was… an exploration.

She could feel it prodding her depths.

Seeking entrance, but to where, she couldn't begin to imagine.

Because she was already crammed so full. Because she was nothing. A blank void remade to suit the whims of a behemoth.

Gills clattered above her.

Schlick-clap.

It was a ragged sound. Labored.

His anatomy not suited for the land. Each breath an obvious struggle for a creature meant to rule the deep.

But still, he remained motionless. Lodged inside her as she rippled and twitched.

Achingly hard.

Still, except for the beat of a thunderous heart and the burrowing exploration of a sentient tube of flesh.

The squirming inside grew more insistent. Pressing against the backside of her navel, it bulged and squished. Prehensile, it pulsed. Growing fat and alien.

And then it coiled against the mouth of her womb.

Horror eclipsed the fog of ecstasy. A cold slap of primal realization that struck Kore with the force of a crashing wave.

Her belly—already tight with rippling climax she hadn't known to expect—was swollen. Bulging where she was stuffed too full of cock. Tight with fluttering muscle clenching in ecstasy as she was filled.

A threat.

An ominous whisper of just how vulnerable a female body truly was.

Reacting without thought, she tried to buck the truth. Tried to flee, even as her body reeled and twitched. Weeping from both ends, her thigh throbbed with a lurch where she'd been stabbed.

The venom.

It coursed through her blood. Wreaking untold havoc on her fragile system. Enough that she'd been subdued with little effort. Ripened against her will. Sullied and tarnished to be...

To be bred by a beast.

He was hard inside her. Impossibly so. Unleashed but unspent.

Thrumming low in his chest, he hummed. A sound beyond hearing laced with pleasure. Amusement.

He moved. At last. As if he'd been waiting for her to recover from the shame of peaking at his command, so he could relish the fight when it flooded her limbs once more.

Scales rasped against the stone. Catching what little light there was, iridescent scales sparkled across the ceiling.

Withdrawing, she was turned out as his hips moved. Claws prickled against the flesh of her upturned bottom, he plunged back inside with a merciless stroke. Using his weight against her, he plundered what had been meant for Apollo. Desecrating that sacred gift.

Breath growing rough and strained outside of his element, he began to work. Pumping her with steady, deliberate strokes that rocked her forward on the cold stone. Every cruel retreat dragged sensitive, clinging flesh with it.

It was a betrayal.

A schism of body and mind, a rift torn wider with every thrust. Her every nerve ignited with a firestorm of feeling that twisted through her limbs. Tracing the bowl between her hips as she was hollowed out and overfilled.

Kore's jaw flexed as she ground her teeth. Eyes squeezed shut as she raged against the shame. The horror. Her mind flooded with the sound of flesh meeting scales, in a damp place that echoed. Heart racing, she was caught between fear and some-thing... worse. An unwelcome, electric thrill borne from every stroke. With every shift of something vital inside her that was shoved aside as the beast made space for himself.

Humid breath dampened her ear, then. Making her cringe as he took a ragged breath at her nape and snarled as he fucked her. It was a primal sound. Low and raw. That of a creature not meant for the land.

Kore shuddered beneath him. Bones turning liquid, she submitted with a squeal.

It was an unconscious thing. Accidental. An unspoken command she obeyed without thought, for it resonated deep within her bones.

Her reward was pleasure.

Blinding. Coiled and deadly.

"Gods, pl-please," Kore gasped, sweating freely as she was worked over that cock. The glide easy. Inviting. Her thighs tacky with spilled cream that splattered against her belly with every impact of scales on skin. And her voice. It cracked when she whispered, "Please," and wasn't sure who might hear her.

She was a vessel.

Empty.

Meant to be filled.

Used.

A plaything for the gods, who ignored her pleas for help, but took everything she might give.

Jaws hanging slack, eyes glassy as she stared into the sightless gloom, Kore mewled when the beast denied her. Resenting even an inch of separation from that divine cock, she tried to chase. Knees bruised when she pushed back, grunting when he dove back in and sealed their bodies together with a grotesque slap and forced the air from her lungs.

Kore took it.

Because she was empty.

Listening to sordid sounds echo inside the cavern, she was sullied. Desecrated. And when the fat, slick head nuzzled against her womb with pulsing interest, she felt a sucking kiss latch against her very last barrier.

And she did nothing.

Because she couldn't.

Because she was a vessel.

A thing to be filled. To endure when her gates were battered, over and over and over again. Each thrust a promise.

She could feel it in the brutal stretch. The rippling veins and slick brine leaking from her gaping cunt, where she'd been ruined and stuffed with the obscene.

And she could hear it in the way his breathing had grown ragged and rough. Each inhale a labour as his gills strained against cutting, waterless air.

With a snarl, he came.

It wasn't like the slaver, with his snappy, jilting pumps of watery seed.

It was nothing like the priest with his cooing pleasantries and doughy, clinging praises.

This was savage.

Snarling above her, the beast opened the floodgates and poured the ocean inside her.

The first spurt splashed inside with enough force to leave her breathless—she felt the molten lash as it sprayed against her end.

Her lips parted around a wordless scream as he swelled, twitching and lurching. A flood pouring out of him in hot, gushing waves that shuddered with every brutal impact of greedy hips as he fought to cram as much of that impossible girth inside her sacred walls.

But he didn't stop.

Not when slime began to pour from stretched lips. Not when molten cream bubbled and dripped with an audible splat against grimy stone.

No, he worked all the harder. Rumbling deep in his chest, huffing against her nape, he shuddered as he spilled. Every serpentine inch of him. Grinding in tight circles, using her to milk himself dry, he clutched her hips and held her in position.

And his cock?

It clung inside. Seeking entrance, it prodded and burrowed. Alive.

Desperate to plant itself where it might never be removed.

Panting through sagging lips, Kore tried to process her new reality. Tried to marry the burn of her every muscle as she quivered with fatigue, with the pulsing, desperate need for more.

Her mind boggy and soaked with confusion as pleasure ignited in her very blood and set fire to her nerves.

Crooning now, the beast burrowed deeper. Letting his cock flail against her womb, until a sharp lance found its mark.

"Unnghhh," Kore squealed, hands desperately clawing at the stone. Some delayed instinct to self-preservation that was aborted with another cruel pump.

And then it began.

She felt it rise through his shaft.

Hot.

Liquid.

It gushed inside her.

Deep inside.

At first, it was just that. Fluid sprayed in great, heaving torrents.

But it didn't stop.

She felt it in the ache where her womb was stretched. Cramping and overfull, she groaned as she was inflated. Her insides rippling with a wanton pulse of betrayal that beckoned him to drive deeper. To keep filling her with every last drop.

There was a pause.

A moment of silence hovered between breaths.

And then, a low, satisfied groan rumbled from an inhuman chest before something ballooned at his base. Where he was wedged between ruined petals. Something that tried to plug what had been pumped inside, and made slick, sensitive walls gape.

Eyes rolling white, Kore felt it. Above the searing pressure making her heavy. Bloated and swollen.

"No!" she screamed, sobbing as she was filled. Fighting against the urge to succumb beneath the piping hot torrent of seed, raging against the command to submit or be drowned in that unnatural ocean. Cunt spasming as it was stretched further still, she wasn't sure if she'd been struck by another mythic peak or if she was convulsing in some kind of demonic fit as he worked to fill her with every last drop of seed.

He ignored her pleas.

Because he was a beast.

Rumbling low in his chest, he sent agonizing spurts into the depths of her very womb, until her belly sloshed with it.

She was helpless but to take it. Swept away.

And when he growled, when the sound of carnal satisfaction rumbled through her very bones, it was a possessive thing that left no room for hope as her opening was stretched.

Scales shimmered in the dim light, a fractal shimmer radiating across the ceiling.

A coil of muscle shifted in his tail, and he shuddered as he bore down. Length twitching as he swelled. Cum gushing with less vigour now, but enough that her womb ached.

"Apollo..." she murmured as the fight bled from her muscles, and the only light she could see was reflected from gleaming scales. "Please... don't..."

A haunting sound crashed against her nape. A sound meant for the deep, one that left her liquid as he wrenched away. Tearing himself free with a howl of pain.

He left her.

Serpentine coils limping back, out of the cave. Back to the shore, where the crash of waves welcomed him.

Gaping, empty, Kore was abandoned. Twice, for without the monster, she was plunged back into the dark.

Left with only the chill of his absence, the shame of need still fluttering where she'd been ruined, and...

... and a belly full to bursting.

63

CHAPTER 10

*B*eneath the cold black waters, deep in the trench at the bottom of the noxious Black Sea, Nyx could finally breathe.

His reef was thriving, pumping oxygenated water into the most poisonous layer of his new kingdom, while the pressure of the deep wrapped around him in a frigid, blissful embrace. Saltwater poured through his gills in great, gasping pulls, chasing the last sting of surface air from his ravaged lungs.

Flexing his tail with a hiss, he let his spines drag through the silt where he was coiled in the shadows. Gills flaring wide and bloody as the last of the surface's stink was purged from his senses.

Except for *her*.

She lingered in every salty breath. The taste of that gushing cunt was sweet where it clung to his palate.

He'd feasted, but each taste had only made him more ravenous.

Unfulfilled, despite the way her dainty little belly had bulged around the sheer volume he'd dumped inside that precious womb.

And the way her tiny human slit had rejoiced? Gushing as he'd forced her to open, milking him with greedy, sucking pulls?

He shuddered in the cool, blissful dark.

Perfection.

Thick and bloated, his cock lurched at the memory. Interest piqued, it snaked free of his slit. Already drooling in the cooling waters. Unsatisfied, for he'd been cut off—denied before she could be bred properly.

Before he could plant his knot behind her pelvic shelf and rut her for hours as they drifted through the currents that answered only to him.

Nyx flashed the edge of pointed, deadly teeth.

She was… human. Fragile. Pathetic. Weak and delicate.

And yet, she'd taken almost all of it. Her dainty pussy—smattered in sparse, brown hair instead of scales—had stretched to accommodate what he'd forced her to take.

But he'd stopped short of knotting her.

Torn himself from that silky grip before he could ruin her.

It was agony.

Sperm belched from his slit, sending silky ribbons snaking into the frigid black.

He'd been forced to leave her there. Drenched in brine, ruined, unconscious, and gaping wide open. Her womb flooded, her body half-claimed. Rosy cheeks of a plump, upturned bottom, hers was a chalice filled to overflowing. A foamy mess bubbling and frothing down her thighs.

But the lock that would bind them? The anchor of flesh that would entwine her soul to the sea remained uncast. Denied by the limits of her disgusting humanity.

She was too soft. Too fragile.

And *he…* he couldn't tolerate hours above the surface—the bloody red mist curling about him in the trench was proof enough of that.

So there'd been no other choice.

He'd fought the urge to knot her until the very end—until his lungs burned, his gills bled, his mind blurring as the poisonous surface air nearly suffocated the life from his chest. Until he'd felt it bloom.

His knot.

Swelling at his base, already forming inside that tight human sheath.

It was a splash of cold terror. Simply a matter of instinct—to set an anchor and seal his seed inside before the ocean might wash it away. As he would with any female of his kind. A *Virelii.*

But this female was not of his kin. Her body not meant to handle what he was driven to do to her.

What he was *going* to do inside her.

Not yet.

No, *this time*, with *this* bride, he'd be deliberate. Careful. Each drop of venom measured before it was pumped into her veins. Applied with dedicated intention as he guided her through the coming shift from pathetic to glorious.

Tongue snaking out, Nyx tasted the darkness. Lips twitching in something that might have been mistaken for a smile.

But wasn't.

For it wouldn't be long. Not long before he might watch her molt that revolting human weakness, and then?

Oh, then he'd drag her beneath the waves and knot her so violently the seven kingdoms would know that Nyxarion Korrides, last of the Abyssari-born kings, exiled to the Black Sea, had claimed a female. One fit to rule the anoxic ocean as his consort. His bride. One he'd *made* to suit an environment none of the *Pelagorn* had ever been able to conquer.

Not quite a *Virelii.*

Not a woman.

She'd be both.

A Siren.

But she wasn't ready.

Not yet.

Claws flexing against the sea floor, he willed his cock to retract. Straining to ignore the agony of a knot denied, he tried to force it back into his vent, behind the protective scales guarding his genital slit.

As if in defiance, a ribbon of seed gushed from his tip, for he could still feel her. Her tight heat fluttering around his girth, the way she'd writhed beneath him. Fighting until her cries had bled into soft mewls of surrender. Crooning as he'd pumped her full of seed...

She'd taken him *so well*.

Come for him when he filled her.

And he'd abandoned her.

Hissing, fins flaring, he scowled at the surface twinkling in the distance and took his cock in a deadly fist. Stroking it as he glared at that hated, burning light.

He needed time to recover. Time for his lungs to heal from the putrid rot above, so he could return with a vengeance. He needed to feed the reef, to let the polyps drink from his venom glands and feast on his blood to ensure it was bound to his will.

He didn't have time to return.

There was work to be done to prepare for his bride...

Knot pulsing in his palm, Nyx snarled. A dull throb of frustration that could only be satisfied inside a pussy gushing slick.

Tail flicking, the barbs in his fins trailed through the silt.

What would it hurt? To return before he was ready. To let the reef hunger for just a little longer. He couldn't drag her from that cave, plunge her fragile human body into the surf, and force his knot back inside—not yet—but she could take just a little more...

Gills flaring wide, a jet of milky seed drifted through the current.

He reacted.

Body coiled, he launched off the sea floor with a violent flick of his tail. Leaving the trench that was now free of the killing, anoxic waters that had defined the Black Sea for millennia, he cut through the silt with a wild, desperate grace. He drove toward the surface, breath a steady, controlled exhale. Through the corrosive layer rich with bacterial decay, through the death-threshold where warm met cold, and very little survived. He shut his second lids and surged through the salinity sheets with a single thought in mind.

Her.

Chasing her scent.

Blind to reason, to the very real threat of his own looming death, he rose. Breaking the surface, his massive body crashed against the rocks. Soggy air searing his tender gills, he flashed pointed teeth as the sea's buoyancy abandoned him once more. His every movement a violent, deliberate act.

The tide was low. His timing poor. The path to his bride rocky and cruel, resistant to his tricks. Unforgiving. His coils scraped stone, spines catching on jagged rock.

He loathed it.

The light. His own colossal weight. The pain of unfiltered air ripping through his gills.

But her scent.

It screamed for him.

And so he persisted.

Dragging his bulk forward, the image of a tiny human pussy glazed with his cum was a beacon he couldn't ignore or resist.

The cave was as he left it.

Tide low, dank and dark and desolate.

And *her.*

A tiny slip of a thing dressed in rags. Collapsed on her left side, her cunt on lewd display. Every inch of her skin bathed in bruises and etched in venom—he could see his mark, just there, pulsing beneath her skin. Coursing through her veins. A glow her pathetic human eyes couldn't perceive.

Not yet.

And her belly.

His breath caught.

It was swollen and grotesque. Bulging around the copious seed he'd pumped inside.

She hadn't spilled a drop.

Snaking closer, Nyx hefted his bulk across the damp stone. Fascinated by the implication. That she could hold so much in such a small body, the greedy little thing.

Realization struck him, then.

There was a difference. Between this bride and the last.

His first had been kept in the warm waters of a secluded lagoon, on the coast of the Aegean Sea. Every drop he'd given her washed away before his mark could sink in.

But this girl.

In keeping her dry, he'd stumbled into success. The air reacted with his cream, clotting and growing solid.

A thick plug.

Seed that had gone from liquid to gel had hardened inside her without the sea to wash it away. What had once gushed from him in torrents had grown thick and unyielding. A barrier so she might cling to the stamp of ownership she had yet to truly earn.

Something possessive rumbled in his chest, then. Something starving for more.

She twitched at the sounds rumbling from his barrel chest, but that was all.

Claws clattering over stone, he ached to touch. To possess. To finish what he'd started and replace that blockage of solidified cum with his knot.

Tracing the flare of her hip, careful not to break delicate skin, he marvelled at the hint of elegant blue lines. Veins flush with venom, glowing from within with his stain.

Looming, cut from obsidian and salt, Nyx blinked at his captive. His ward. Ignoring the burn of air in his lungs, for the sight before him was one to eclipse all discomfort.

Beautiful.

But he hadn't come to merely look.

Careful, he peeled gooey petals apart and twisted one clawed finger inside tender walls. Catching the plug of solidified seed on that pointed, vicious hook, he tugged it free with deliberate, tiny movements.

A faint sound slipped from her lips, but that was all. Even as the cum gushed from her depths, she was still. Pliant. Ready to be bred once more.

Gripping his cock in a fist that commanded obedience, Nyx fed that bloated length through the sopping mess and set his crown to her entrance.

He waited. Just for a moment. Just long enough to admire the way swollen lips yawned wide enough to swallow his tip. A preverse thrill made his spines flare when his seed bubbled at her seam, making her slick and gooey.

Pressing his weight into her, he took. Flexing to send his cock through the mess, Nyx crammed his girth through a tight band of muscle.

Bliss.

She parted for him with a sigh. Welcoming, impossibly soft—*tight*—she gripped him like she'd been made to take him. And still, she did not wake.

She merely spasmed around him. Unconscious as a helpless orgasm wracked her tiny body while she lay pliant beneath him.

Grunting, Nyx shivered at such a welcome.

It was a marvel to see such a thing. Fragile, bloodless lips stretched white around his girth. Accommodating his invasion, even now. Without conscious thought.

She fluttered in welcome. Arched when he struck her end, and clenched as he bore down, seeking to penetrate her womb and pump his spawn inside.

Claws bracketing her hips, he worked her over his shaft,

driving into her with punishing force just to see if he could wake her from her stupor.

But her eyes merely rolled white.

Low, ragged grunts of pleasure echoed with the wet slap of scales on skin. Her legs twitching with every merciless thrust he shoved inside.

A riptide boiled in his balls. Climax rising in a violent surge, he fucked what he'd claimed and let it take him.

Take them both.

Nyx snarled as he came, balls flexing as he dumped every ounce of wrath and frustration into her body. His hatred toward her kind. The rage of injustice for what had been done to him. And the hope for what she would become.

All of it.

His massive body collapsed atop hers, cock wriggling where her womb tried to deny what was already his. Barbing out, a spigot lanced from his tip and forced her cervix to widen as if she were one of his kind. A *Virelii* female meant to handle a *Pelagorn* male in all his glory.

But she was human.

Still…

Fins shivering in full flare, Nyx pulsed inside her, unloading thick ropes of sperm. Making her bulge once more—he felt it happen. Snaked one hand beneath her to hold her belly as it grew swollen and taut. Skin stretching to accommodate the obscene volume pouring from his balls.

Nyx rumbled, crooning for her. His bride.

Dizzy with the rush of release, he tugged free of that blissful, silken grip before his knot could ruin her. Taking his cock in a clawed fist, the other hand still cupping a belly ripe with his cum, he pumped the last ropes of seed across her upturned bottom.

Marvelling at the lash of pearly seed that splattered across rosy skin, for even as he watched, it changed.

Reacting with the hated surface air, his cum hardened into a gelatinous rope.

And he grinned.

This one would survive.

Undone by her own nature, her own inability to survive beneath the waves, where his sperm might be washed away. Instead, she'd be exposed to his toxin, even while he was forced to retreat, lurking in the trench until he'd recovered enough to fuck her to overflowing once more.

Panting, gills straining, he stayed long enough to watch the plug form inside her. Long enough to ensure that she wouldn't waste a single drop, until the urge to breed her was overcast by burning lungs and ravaged gills.

For now, she was full. Stuffed.

Claimed.

His bride would wake alone, *yes*, but she wouldn't be without him.

And the next time he broke the surface?

He'd come with the tide.

And nothing would hold him back…

CHAPTER 11

linking in the gloom, Kore lay still. Wrapped in a heavy blanket of silence. The only signs of life the rise and fall of her chest. A faint flutter beneath the corner of her jaw.

She was alone. It was there in the quiet.

The hush.

Her every muscle aching and sore, her sex still fluttering with the unspeakable things that had been done to it... but... she was alone.

Breath shallow, each inhale a struggle against some immense pressure she couldn't fathom as she was. Lying prone in a pool of slime and shame. A grotesque echo she refused to acknowledge.

Instead, she squeezed her eyes shut and tried to breathe through the shame.

Outside, beyond the cave, the tide splashed against the shore. Calling for her. A beckoning. For her surrender.

It was an offer of oblivion, if only she might slip beneath the waves and let go.

But it was a lie.

A cruel temptation, for she knew better now. The sea was a hunting ground, and she... she was nothing but prey.

The cave pressed in around her. At once too small, too damp, too close, and yet... cavernous. Pulsing with a sinister heat not her own. Her skin scraped raw—nipples, knees, elbows, and cheek—from the unforgiving kiss of the stone floor, and a grip of prickling, unrelenting cruelty. Her ears fuzzing with the scream of silence that echoed with obscene memory.

And her lips. They tasted of salt. Blood. The particular flavor of her pleas where they still lingered on her palate, the way she'd begged for relief—from torment or for more, she couldn't bring herself to say.

But her belly.

She didn't want to look.

So her hand moved instead. Trembling, sliding across feverish skin, until she encountered the swell.

Still there.

Still achingly full.

Proof that the impossible was real. That she'd begged a god— her god—to save her, but another had answered. A darker one.

A leviathan.

From the deep.

A beast with a single thought, driven by primal instinct to breed female flesh. Willing or not.

Her hand slid lower, toward the slick throb pounding between her legs.

A gasp shattered the oppressive silence, then.

Swollen, slippery skin came alive at the slightest touch. Her mound was raw, gooey with something that slipped but couldn't be wiped away. Gelatinous ropes hardened where they'd been left to dry.

But her clit?

It screamed.

Her core clenching around a plug of something solid, she couldn't help but trace that sensitive bundle of bulbous nerves.

A tiny climax shuddered through her. Hardly provoked, a

thing she'd never experienced before the beast—not even in the divine chambers of Apollo's consecrated holy men. Those chosen to spill virgin blood across the altar in the heart of Delphi.

It was the venom.

She knew.

Even through the haze of climax, her fingers a fumbling blur of desperation, she knew—how unnatural this fog really was. That if she'd been meant to climb such a delirious peak for any, it should have been the holy men who served Apollo.

And yet...

Kore could feel it moving through her blood, whispering the secrets of the sea through her veins. Throbbing in time with the pulse pounding in her sex.

Too depleted to cry, she squeezed her eyes shut and saw a flash in the sparkling dark. A canvas on which to paint her torment, where she couldn't escape. Fragments of something sinister danced just beyond her grasp. The weight of that impossible body atop hers, scales grating against her skin.

And the relentless thrust of an inhuman cock filling her.

"Gods," she whispered. Had he returned to her? Taking advantage of helpless flesh while she'd been enthralled in the grip of unconsciousness? "No," she rasped, denying it. It was the venom playing tricks. Nothing more.

Gritting her teeth, she tried to push herself up. Tried to flee, and only managed to stagger and slip. She collapsed, the impact sending a ripple of movement sloshing through her. It was as if the very sea itself had been pumped inside her, churning with the fury of the tides.

"No," she said again, teeth bared. Determination scrawled across her brow. She would not give in—a priestess of Apollo was trained to resist the dark, and so she would fight it to her very last breath.

A gull cried. Drawing her slitted gaze to the world outside these desecrated walls.

Night. It had begun to blanket all her eyes could see. Everything they couldn't.

And she was alone.

Baring her teeth, ears popping as she clenched her jaw, Kore fought to stand. Despite the throbbing, tender flesh begging for relief, the bruises and chaffed skin, and the belly full of poisonous cum. Sweating, breath coming in great, heaving gulps, she claimed her feet and wobbled in the dusk.

"Just one step," she whispered to no one, because there was only the dark. "Just take one, single step."

It was a challenge that nearly toppled her. Her center of balance sent her heaving too far forward. Hands flying out, she clung to the cave wall, fingers hooked into claws. Protecting her belly, where it protruded before her.

Sweat ran in tacky rivulets down her temples, soaking her hair. But she persisted as she'd been taught. Clawing her way out, she left the cave where she'd been fucked by a beast, and collapsed in the sand with a cry of triumph.

The tide splashed against the shore. Mocking her. Each lapping wave pushed a little higher as the sea encroached. Foamy peaks capped with the dying sun, stained purple and crimson.

She stayed until the sweat cooled and dried on her skin, replaced by the kiss of seafoam and dew. Stayed until the sun slipped beneath the waves and drowned in the distant sea.

Motionless. Her limbs aching with the burden of the beast's venom, his sperm and cruel grip... but most of all, it was the weight of her own complicity.

Her shame.

"I'm sorr—"

Choking, she couldn't bring herself to say it. Couldn't muster the apology because she had no idea where she could even begin to atone for what she'd done.

So she sat in the surf. Staring as the tide rose to lave at her toes, kissing her shins… suckling at her knees. She stayed until her thighs prickled with foam splashing across the shore.

Only then did she scramble back. Shocked back into herself by the knowledge that he was still out there. Lurking where she could not see.

That he was not finished with her.

Not yet.

"I am a priestess of Delphi," she whispered. Forcing steel into her blood, Kore stood and scowled at the surf. "And I will not be taken."

She needed a weapon. Some method to defend herself against a god.

Food. Water.

Resources that would enable her defiance—anything and everything she might use as a means to resist.

Trembling, Kore shook off the daze. Hands cupping the swell of her inflated belly, swaying in the dark, she paused. Took a breath. And turned her back on the sea. Tugging the scraps of her robes around her nudity, she concealed puffy nipples from the bite of chilly wind and trudged through the sea foam, determined to master the haunting dark.

It was a slog.

A brutal trek through wet sand, limping to avoid overusing her wounded leg still throbbing with venom, she set her eyes to the eastern end of the island and began to march. Pacing the water's edge, she hauled her swollen belly. Her eyes flicking through the dark as she explored her prison. This lonely spit of land in the heart of some unknown sea.

But there was nothing. Nothing but a limestone hill, a beach, and a cave sliced into stone from aeons of crashing tidal waves.

It took her less than two hundred paces to find the edge of the beach—she counted. Encountering crumbling boulders vanishing beneath the waves. Treacherous in full daylight, but at night? Without so much as a sliver of moon to guide her way?

She whimpered.

Hugging her rags around herself, she took a trembling breath and turned back.

But the Western limit was much the same, only here, the wind slapped her face and mocked her tears, sending her stumbling back to the beach.

There was only the cave itself. Cut into stone, a sheer face of rock. A hysterical laugh bubbled from her lips, for she stumbled toward the only whisper of freedom with a single thought in her foggy head.

The beast was enormous.

A master of his element, *yes*, utterly uncontested. But here? On land? Such a creature could not climb.

Kore rushed toward the rock wall. Where gulls had gathered sticks to hold their eggs, where they might watch the trials below from lofty perches. Bleary-eyed in the night.

She scrambled atop a boulder, standing on the balls of her feet. Fingers outstretched, she grasped the biting edge of a hand-hold and tried to heft herself up.

But she was ungainly.

Weak from drowning and fucking.

Heavy from… everything else.

She fell. Crashing back to the unforgiving earth in a puddle of bruised and swollen flesh. A pathetic heap of limbs splashing into frigid wet.

The impact sent a new pain shooting through her, then. Bright and distracting, a new bruise to add to the rest. One she hardly bothered to notice, for the ache in her cum-crusted seam…

… and the water.

It had risen while she'd fumbled through the night.

The tide sloshed at her knees, almost flooding the cave.

"Gods," she whispered. Horrified by the realization. "No…"

It was right there.

Rising.

Already.

A hint of how this cave had come to be in the first place, the water was surging higher with every pulse of the sea. Chasing her back inside, she scrambled free of the surf and headed for higher ground.

Clambering into the dark, screeching as the water chased her, she went for higher ground. Reduced to little more than a primitive animal fleeing for whatever meager scrap of safety might be claimed.

Panic lent her agility, despite her injuries and her girth, for she was a girl born of the mountains, once. Bred to serve in the temple that reached for the sky, where jagged rock baked in the everlasting sun.

Knees crashing into stone, Kore collapsed in the same place she'd begun. Where she could still smell the scent of seed and brine. And she knew…

… the beast would return with the tide.

Curling around her toes, her belly rolling with sloshing cum, she hiccuped. "Nooo," she breathed. Cringing. Trying to keep her skin free of the encroaching sea. "Please… Please, I can't…"

But it was too late.

Already, the water swirled around her ankles, making her flinch at the touch that was both icy and searing hot. Skin prickling with a shower of gooseflesh, a keening wail assaulted her vocal cords.

And then, "Not again," she murmured, eyes glazed by a fog of panic. Seeing what wasn't there, but would come again. "Not again. *Please.* B-By Ap-Apollo," she stammered, fingers trying to twist into patterns already fading from memory, instead, daring to speak her Lord's name for the first time since she'd drowned and summoned another. "I beg you. Let me be."

It was futile.

A plea drowned by the crash of lapping waves.

Mocking her, the surf lapped at her calves, soaking her ragged robes to lick at blotchy, water-logged skin.

She didn't notice.

Rigid with fear, Kore could only stare into the dark. Flinching at every tiny sound. Seeing the glint of scales in the peak of every wave. The glimmer of the moon sent her cowering deeper in the dark.

Heart hammering in her chest, trying to break through rib and tear muscle from the bone.

There was nowhere to run. No place he couldn't reach her.

The beach was gone.

She was trapped.

"My Lord," she rasped, and let any remaining scraps of pride float away in the surf. "Please. I'll do any-anything. *Anything.*"

Her offer went unanswered.

Because she was nothing.

Once a consecrated priestess of Apollo, and now... merely a vessel. One claimed for a monstrous ritual. Passed from god to god, a plaything for divine whims.

Hot tears tracked down her cheeks, only to be lapped up by the sea.

The tide had risen. Swallowed her hips and teased her navel.

"I can't do it again," she murmured, shivering in the gloom. "I can't take any more."

But she could.

Icy liquid fingers slipped inside her, the water invasive in a way nothing else could possibly be. Scouring the monster's cum from inside her, it dissolved the plug keeping her bloated with sperm.

With a gush, the dam burst.

Seed surged from her cunt in a torrent of shame and profound relief.

"Ahhh—" Kore screamed, back arching, clumsy fingers flying

to cup her bruised pussy as the monster's cream gushed from deep inside.

Climax rippled through her flesh. And with eyes bulging in the dark, Kore watched an oil slick shimmer atop the surface before it was swallowed by churning waves.

Leaving her empty.

Ready...

... for...

... *more*...

CHAPTER 12

$\mathcal{H}$e watched from the waves. Clinging to the sea's embrace, content to observe as the little female wandered the back of the cave, her belly no longer swollen. Pacing the edge of the tide, avoiding the water as if it might save her to remain dry. As if she had any hope of escape.

Delicate hands plucked at detritus left at the edge of the tide. Strands of battered kelp. Crabs dancing in shallow tidal pools. Pressing crustaceans and kelp to cracked, dehydrated lips, she ate. Like a savage.

A starving thing.

Her attempts were pitiful.

Almost… charming in a primitive manner.

So much that at first, he wasn't sure what she was doing. Not until she took a bit of greenery between her lips and began to chew. Her nose scrunched in disgust.

A cute, wrinkled pucker.

But a shameful attempt at survival, nevertheless.

"Please," she murmured, her voice carrying through the waves as she licked salt from her fingers. "A-Apollo… *please*…"

He shivered.

It was a voice laced with exhaustion. Thick with confusion. But a voice rich in something he couldn't name. Something beautiful and grotesque. Something human and... *more.*

A hint of what was to come.

Until then...

She moaned, curling into herself. Body wracked by shivers as she clutched at a flat belly.

His bride hungered.

A grin kissed his lips, then. Sinister, cruel, it was a thing that made the water still, just for a moment, for even at this distance, he could see it.

The glow.

Pulsing through her veins. Surging beneath her skin.

It called to him. A beacon he couldn't resist.

And so, he began to hum.

The Resonance.

It began in his chest, a tectonic friction, a sound utterly beyond her pathetic human ears. A sound she couldn't hear...

... because it was meant for her body.

Using the water, he sent a vibration through the surf. A song older than the Wind. More ancient than the Earth. Older even than the Fires that sank beneath the waves so many eons ago.

The water shivered.

Shaking the sand, he made each grain dance, turning the shore into something treacherous for land-dwellers.

Easing his passage.

Taking one final pull through his gills, he slid from the water. Crooning a sound beyond hearing, he purred as he breached the surf, dragging coils of glittering, wet muscle ashore. Serpentine as he slid through quicksand with relative ease. His every movement fluid, timed to land with the waves rolling gently ashore with the receding tide.

Reacting to the sound, his bride went still before she clenched. Glistening wet thighs slid together as he approached.

She was enthralled by the song of the Black Sea. Obedient. Pliant.

Ready.

Weeping for a mate she could not see, desperate for him to soothe the pain of hunger. To give more of what she craved but couldn't name.

The molten salt of his cum—the serum that would bind her to the sea.

He'd stayed away too long. Took longer than he'd meant recovering his strength in the trench, feeding his foundling reef until his venom sacs were depleted. Long enough for the seal inside her to rupture. For the tide to come and go, carrying the scent of his seed mixed with human slick.

Long enough for her to want…

His bride hungered.

And he could give.

The surface was pain. A dull roar screaming in his gills as the air seared the sensitive filaments not meant to taste pure oxygen. His every breath a chore with a price.

But the sight of her?

Tiny.

Bare.

Gushing for him?

He hefted his enormous bulk from the loving embrace of the sea, for pain was an old lover, and Nyx would not suffer without purpose.

It was sacrifice.

Calculated.

The price he must pay for such a creature as *this.*

Her.

Bracing for the coming marathon, he paused to look.

She lay in shadows, huddled at the back of the cave. Eyes closed, trembling as her body reacted to the Resonance. His purr.

A crease pinched between dainty brows, and her skin? It was laced with the pulsing blue of the deep. She was marked.

His.

Already, she was progressing. Taking to his toxin in a way that promised what she could be. Already further along than her predecessor.

Nyx flashed his teeth, hissing low. Fins flaring at the painful memory.

This one would be different.

Better.

He would take his time. Ensure she consumed enough, flooded her from every direction with venom and seed, bloating her on the essence that would usher her into a new life.

And when she was ready, when the last scrap of her grotesque humanity had been drowned in brine, he would knot her so deep the Black Sea itself would rejoice.

For he would have his queen.

And she would never resurface again.

His song deepened.

With a fluid, monstrous grace of something not meant for land, Nyx entered the cave. Each coil of his tail dragging over stone, leaving a trail of scales where they were torn from his flesh. Bloodied and glittering in his wake.

It was a cold determination to continue. A blanket of fierce need that settled over him as he watched with unblinking, predatory patience.

Plotting.

Cock pressing at his seam, he rumbled deeper.

He'd strip her of every drop of fragile, human instinct. Hollow her out, and remake her into something gorgeous. A creature that would be the envy of the seven seas.

Silent, but for the hiss of his coils on stone, he snaked toward her. Eager to begin. When he was close enough to touch, his cock slithered from his slit with lazy menace. Already leaking, veined and pulsing as a gush of fluid escaped his tip, he reached.

Cupping a taut breast, he tugged at the rosy peak and crooned when she arched into his touch. Rewarding her obedience, he played with her.

The scent of pussy bloomed in the dank, humid air.

Raw and desperate.

For him.

Because she belonged to the sea.

And he was starving too.

With a flick of his tail, he settled beside her. Hefting his tail over her abdomen, he brought forth the smallest spine nestled in a dorsal fin.

One he'd saved for her.

Venom beaded at the tip an instant before he barbed her. Thrumming to keep her docile, crooning as she squirmed at the molten heat pumping into her muscle.

Groaning low, her jaws went slack. "Apollo," she murmured, eyelids flickering in delirium. "My lord, please... take me... *save* me..."

Gills fluttering, Nyx grinned. Pausing to stroke his girth from base to bulging tip, he milked a surge of cum and smeared it across sagging lips.

Her tongue darted out. To taste. To savor.

A breathy groan vibrated through his shaft.

And hazy, glassy eyes fixed to his face. Unfocused, a dazed smile spread across her lips.

Pinching, he twisted that caught nipple and made her squirm. Gave her a tiny fraction of the pain he suffered just to give her this gift, he tortured that swollen bead until it grew puffy and red.

Gaping, she was transfixed.

Her foggy, animal gaze fell to his cock with a gasp. Hypnotized by the ridged and glowing lines, she mapped his girth.

Worshipped what he flexed and sent toward a hole he had yet to defile.

Cum oozed from his tip, the tiny slit belching up a pearly bead.

And, setting one clawed thumb to her pout, Nyx dragged her lips further apart and commanded her to open. To take what only he might give.

Heat.

Blissful, searing heat.

His song stuttered to a halt, his gills flapping with the strain of restraint. And with a rumbling snarl, Nyx buried one fist in tangled, brown hair and pulled her face down on his cock.

Wasting no time, he slithered into her.

Ridges popping through the tight ring of her lips, he made it fit. Flexed, so his girth would thin and reach as far into her throat as he could.

She spluttered.

Offering a weak flail as the song faded from her ears.

But it was much, *much* too late for that.

This was a claiming already begun.

Her mouth was receptive enough that he surged forward in a single, relentless press. Thrilled by the way her throat clenched at his helm, the velvet grasp of a hole created for him to fuck, even if that tight sleeve spasmed in some pathetic attempt at rejection.

She would learn.

Clawing at his scales, she fought—and clenched around him.

Slapping at his belly, she tried to push him back—and massaged his shaft.

The desperate, greedy little thing.

He would oblige her.

Picking up a heavy rhythm, he worked her throat in steady, ruthless strokes. Holding her head in place as her gag reflex surrendered, he plumbed her throat. Offering the tiniest sips of oxygen, for soon she would learn to go without.

Fucking her throat with brutal, measured precision, Nyx used his colossal weight to his advantage. Letting his pearls bulge along his shaft as he neared the end, he adjusted his grip and sent his cock deeper.

She gagged.

Cried.

Moaned.

Her stomach heaved before she relaxed.

Fingers hooked into claws, smoothed out. Stroked what she could reach as she coaxed him toward climax.

She took him, exactly as a bride ought.

Claws flexing against stone, he let his hips snap into her once more before his shaft grew thick and sluggish. Stretching her jaws wide as they might go, he roared. Burying himself in that slender human throat.

And he came.

Sending jet after lashing jet of seed gushing down her throat, he fed his mate. Filling her with endless, punishing pulses.

She choked.

Gurgled.

Swallowing him down in great, heaving gulps, she nursed at his prick. Instinctively. Her belly rounding out with every heated pulse.

Thrumming, he let her feast until she was bloated. Distended and full.

Enormous balls flexing, he groaned with his head thrown back when they too popped from his slit. Displayed against the gleam of his scales, flexing against her chin, he emptied himself.

It was an offer, though she didn't know it.

A gesture between mates to expose so delicate a part of himself to a female, for if she'd been one of his kind—a *Virelii*—she might have been able to resist. As it was...

Her eyes rolled white as she swallowed an obscene torrent of cum, taking everything he could offer until a gurgle whistled through her nostrils.

A tiny moan vibrated up his shaft.

A fragile shudder as she shifted toward him, still hungry for *more.*

It was enough to make him snarl. The complete surrender? The vacant eyes?

She was perfection, his little human slut.

And so, he would not harm her. No matter the ecstasy of her clinging throat, the way her eyes had gone limpid and vacant, this was a feeding.

Unquestionably selfish, *yes.*

But action with purpose.

Pulling back, he pumped a rope of sticky cum across her lips as he pulled his cock free. Leaving her face smeared with a pearlescent sheen, sperm dripping from slack lips, he paused to catch his breath. Toying with her tongue, probing that soft mouth with two fingers, he admired the pretty thing he'd enslaved.

The scent of female slick heated the air with need.

Her need.

Grinning, he pulled his length back, curling it behind his slit, sealing it behind a flap of scales. He sank greedy fingers into the mess between her legs. Parting swollen folds, he filled her. Caressing the place he'd soon bury his knot.

Teasing delicate flesh, making her arch around a belly swollen with him, he felt her clench.

Helpless little human.

She spasmed in an attempt to suck him back inside. The pearl of her clit swollen and needy.

"Please," she groaned, voice raspy with the abuse. Both hands snaking down to strum that knob of female flesh. "I… I need it. It… it hurts… *please…*"

He grinned.

She *wanted* to be bred.

But burning gills and an empty sack spoke of another pressing need—recovery.

Thumbing her clit just to make her buck in his palm, Nyx abandoned her at the height of her need.

Leaving her wanton and wanting.

Tasting fingers saturated in female slime, he purred. Tongue laving up every drop, he licked the salt from his digits, then turned.

Chuckling, he snaked toward the sea. Chasing the tide as it retreated.

Not bothering himself to look back at the creature he'd claimed, Nyx vanished beneath the waves with a satisfied sigh.

Empty balls already beginning to boil anew.

She'd burn while he recuperated.

And the next time he returned...

... she'd beg.

CHAPTER 13

*I*t was obscene, the way her mouth watered for more.

Lifting trembling fingers, Kore painted her lips and found them sticky with cooling ropes of his essence.

She sobbed.

Just once. Enough to acknowledge the horror of what she was doing. Even as that cry became a groan, as her abused nipples tightened, her core clenching at the flavor that burst on her tongue, for with a greedy rush, she'd scooped up every forgotten, humiliating drop and sucked it from her fingers.

Obscene.

Still, she searched.

Fingers tracing the tender bruise he'd left on her jaw, the swell of puffy lips that had stretched around his girth.

All gone.

But his brine lingered on her tongue, hung heavy in the moist air. Clinging to the back of her sinuses, the scent surging in her mind with every fevered breath.

Shifting—thighs slick, pussy swollen and neglected—Kore groaned when her belly sloshed. And when she burped, she tasted an echo of the sea and knew she was already lost.

Her stomach was full. Gurgling with the impossible volume he'd pumped down her throat.

She'd been filled from both ends, now.

Still, something insidious inside her writhed with a ravenous hunger. Begging for... *more.*

Baring her teeth, Kore scowled at the waves. Slapping one hand to stone, she forced her battered body forward. On hands and knees, she crawled. Bottom swaying. Chasing the tide, following the trail of glittering, iridescent scales that led back to the shore.

"*No,*" she snarled, not brave enough to utter more than a defiant whisper. "I reject your claim, son of Poseidon. I was born to serve another."

But the heat of him burned in her gut. Mocking, for she could feel it spreading, took note of the way it twisted through her blood with every beat of her heart.

Eyes fixed to the distant waves, where she'd watched the flick of his tail slip beneath the surface, she heard the sound of cruel laughter ringing in the fog of her memory. Remembered the way he'd pumped her pussy with two fingers and stretched her walls, only to leave her desperate. Empty, despite how recently she'd been... *filled.*

She remembered.

What she'd done.

That she'd nursed at his cock as if his sperm was the very breath she needed to fill her lungs—but she'd done it *willingly.*

Not at first. Not when the panic at having her throat invaded had blinded her with panic... But when the first lash hit the back of her throat? Coating her tongue in an explosion of flavor?

She moaned before her breath caught.

Shame washed over her, then.

But there was something else. Some other fog of memory she dredged from the back of her mind.

As a fish pulled from the sea, she recalled a mist of red from flapping, straining gills not meant to endure the surface air. Moisture that beaded across a proud brow and left a waxy sheen on greying skin. A particular tremble in clawed, clutching hands.

Kore knew suffering—she'd been a vessel for the divine all her life.

And so she knew the beast paid a terrible price to come ashore… to do what he did to her. Knew it without considering, for Kore had been paying the price of serving the divine since the Oracle had fallen.

The price of her sins.

She'd been untouched until the Spartan army had called on Delphi for a miracle. Sacred, until she'd been sampled in front of an audience, bent over an auctioneer's table, and traded for two hundred and sixteen drachmas.

But *they* hadn't made her beg.

Apollo's priest had been kind in his brevity, his identity hidden behind a mask. Tipping her hips back before the thimble of fluid might escape his thin prick.

The slaver had been selfish. Unwashed and cruel, but overcome by her unblemished skin after a few desperate, greedy thrusts. His time inside her was marked by a handful of lusty groans, the clink of silver, and calloused, pawing hands. The only moisture he'd been able to force between her legs, a gob of spittle and a watery dribble of semen.

But this?

Nothing in the scripture could have prepared her for *this*.

One hand circling her throat, Kore shivered. Remembering the stretch. The way the beast had opened her throat with such terrifying ease. The sentient way his cock had reached beyond her limits, growing thin and fat in measured pulses. Surging too far. Withdrawing only enough to set an anchor before reaching again.

And…

And the way she'd swallowed and gulped as he poured the sea down her throat.

A shaft of sunlight danced across the beach, peeking through the clouds. The sun bleeding through, as if to summon her back into the light.

Wordless, guttural sobs broke through the film of composure, then, and she scrambled toward the dancing sunlight. Desperate for the kiss of her Lord's attention. To be saved from this wretched, sodden cave.

She stumbled.

Tripping on wet stone, landing hard on her knees in the shallow, retreating tide, Kore cried out as unfiltered sunlight burned her eyes. Searing pain lanced through her skull, making her whimper as she cowered.

It was accusation.

Punishment for her betrayal.

That, even now, the flesh promised to Apollo was swollen and slick with aching, desperate want of another.

"My Lord," she rasped, voice mangled by the monster who'd fucked her throat raw. "Please... I... I'm sorry."

The sunlight only burned hotter.

Apollo's wrath beat down upon her as she emerged from the dark with a belly full of her carnal betrayal.

Cheeks wet with the congealing salt of her guilt.

Holding one hand out, trying to twist fumbling fingers into some forgotten pattern, she hiccuped through a sob and set her free hand to work. Plunging two fingers down her throat, she gagged. Bringing up what had been so eagerly choked down, she vomited into the surf. Expelling everything she'd swallowed, returning it to the sea from whence it had come, purging until she was left shaking and empty.

Weak.

Exhausted.

The setting sun bled violet and black, streaking the horizon with angry accusation before surrendering to the night once more.

She'd failed.

Again.

Blinking, freed of the pain of searing light, Kore stared at the waves.

She'd failed.

Utterly.

Her prayers had fallen on the wrong ears.

Her skin throbbed with pain from Apollo's rejection, already bubbling where she'd been burned so badly it hurt to simply breathe.

But still, through the fog of heartbreak and delirium, she ached. Throbbing where she'd been defiled. Needy where she'd been made to sample something divine.

Dejected, she stood.

A glow caught her eye.

Faint.

Blue.

Luminous.

It was pulsing through her veins, just beneath the surface of her skin. An eerie light show, both beautiful and… horrifying, for it was a map of something ancient. Wrong.

"Gods," she rasped. "*No.*"

Venom.

She could see it. Knew at a glance that she'd been filled with something so much more insidious than semen.

And with trembling hands, she searched. Touching herself, tracing aching skin, until she found it at the top of her left thigh.

A wound.

Small.

Raised.

Dimpled in the center. A crater where she'd been barbed with another dose of the toxin that had enthralled her so. Deafened her to Apollo's love as she was enslaved to something beyond her comprehension. Something carnal and lewd.

Something that demanded all of her—everything she'd never known to give.

Bluish veins spidered out from the center of that wound. Glowing in the encroaching night.

Clenching around nothing, Kore willed herself to be disgusted by that otherworldly glow. Convulsing around an offensive emptiness, she forced her lips to form around the sacred words of her youth. Trying to summon what had been beaten into her as she knelt at Apollo's altar.

Searching for His warmth in the burn on her skin.

There was only a glowing in the darkness.

Only the quiet roar of the sea as it lapped at the beach.

And the pulse of something primal, deep inside her.

Backing away, her prayers forgotten, Kore fled. Back into the welcoming dark of the cave. Where she'd been defiled and remade. Sullied by a demon with a claim to her body.

"I refuse." It was a denial. A plea. To whom, she couldn't begin to say.

It didn't matter.

She was being tested.

And she was failing.

Miserably.

Wholly.

Breath hitching as a shudder rippled through her muscles, Kore took a breath. Nipples growing taut where they chafed at her tattered robes. Her clit pulsed, full and heavy.

Neglected, where it screamed with a heartbeat of its own. Demanding she submit.

Hands pressed between her thighs, she slid down the cave wall with a trembling whine. Back scraped raw where she'd been burned by a god's wrath, she tried to stem the tide of arousal howling through her nerves. Singing in time with the thrashing of a broken heart.

It hadn't been enough to simply take her body. To corrupt her so fully that her hands strayed, even as she whispered, "This isn't me." And her fingers sank through the slippery mess oozing from her battered pussy as her claims of denial were chased off by a trembling, guttural moan.

She remembered.

The way he'd strummed her aching pearl as he'd plumbed her throat, then abandoned her to the dark without a backward glance.

She could recall the exact timber of his booming laugh as he'd slithered from the cave, leaving a trail of scales and slime that mocked her pain. The ache of denial.

And she knew everything else… had memorized his taste, his smell, the sounds he made as he came so violently that she knew what it was to drown in a god's lust.

A wave of dizziness struck her as her fingers worked. An animal without thought. A female in heat trying to relieve the bubble of pressure building between the cradle of her hips. Fire washed through her pelvis, leaving her skin too tight. The nerves too sensitive and screaming with the want of a beast.

He'd come back.

No matter the pain or the price, she knew he'd come again.

This was no mindless leviathan who rutted at every vulnerable female slit to drown in the Aegean Sea.

He'd come because he had a plan. Designs upon her body that didn't stop at working the seam between her legs for his own morbid pleasure.

He wouldn't stop until he had every last piece of her. Not until he'd stolen her away from her Lord, bit by bit, until she was little more than this awful, throbbing need.

The glow under her skin was proof enough of that.

This map of betrayal he'd injected into her blood.

Climax washed through her as her hands squelched through the mess. Slipping off her clit as her digits became a desperate blur.

Too much.

Not enough.

Sweat soaked her hairline as she gasped in the gloom and came apart at the memory of his cock inside her. Heart pounding between her legs, in the hush of the cave's dark embrace.

Clarity ebbed as the fever of that heat began to clear.

Because this *wasn't* her. This all-consuming drive to reach that mysterious peak, to be stretched and stuffed.

It was the venom.

Slit still throbbing, she focused on her ragged breath. Matching it with the sound of the tide rushing in and out. Lulling her into the state of torpor she'd been trained to endure for another. That trance-like state expected of Apollo's chosen few trained to catch glimpses of the future and deep, forgotten past.

There, she found calm in the heart of a tempest. The knowing of an Oracle in training.

The beast had a plan.

A mission.

Designs upon her body.

A claim to her mind and a stake in her body.

He meant to corrupt her—to what end, she couldn't say. Only that it was devastatingly successful in driving her away from the heat of her Lord's divine grace.

But Kore was a priestess.

Forged in suffering. Disciplined in the art of submission to a force greater than even the sea.

And so, her patience would become her weapon.

She was a vessel for the divine. A chalice designed to be filled, so the gods might drink. Her body had *never* been hers, not wholly.

The moon cast a silver light across the mouth of the cave, hinting at lush curves and puffy peaks concealed within.

She was an offering. Empty. Nothing but a lure meant to draw the creatures of the deep ashore. A sacrifice to the divine.

As she'd always been.

Understanding brought clarity, and with it, a sense of calm washed away the dread.

It was nothing to submit, not really. Not when the force she tried to fight was unbeatable, as undeniable as the coming tide.

He would come again, and this time, Kore would let him invade. Welcome his assault with parted thighs and a graceful smile that hid what lurked beneath the surface.

Rebellion.

Tracking the passage of time between breeding sessions, she'd surrender herself to the moon. Use the tide to mark the days, just as he used it to mark *her*.

And then?

Her body was already lost, but her mind? It would stay sharp. Cutting and disciplined, as she'd been molded to be. A ceremonial blade meant for dark ritual beyond the comprehension of mortal vision.

Venom pulsed beneath her skin. Twitching in her muscles. Calling her to the shore.

She stood, piling stones beneath the surface of the water to mark the tide, then let the venom use her feet, bleary gaze fixed to the distant waves.

A plan. She had a plan.

The venom pulsed.

Her feet moved.

Blue light gushed through her veins.

He was coming.

And this time, she'd be ready…

CHAPTER 14

*E*ye all but vacant, Kore walked.

Feet stumbling. Hands limp at her sides. Nudity peaking through tattered rags, her flesh jiggled as she trudged through wet sand.

"I... I am... the chalice," she murmured, her tone flat, despite the rasp in her voice where she'd been fucked raw.

Her feet splashed into the surf.

"I am Kore Dionari, of the divine flame, and I am the chalice," she said again, stronger now, as she went to her knees. Skin throbbing where she'd been burned by the wrath of a sun god, cooled by the embrace of the sea. Chasing relief, Kore lay on damp sand and sighed as her thighs fell apart. The scorched skin of her back was soothed by the cool sand, scoured clean by the salt, no matter the burn.

Bathed in moonlight and seafoam, she exposed all that was swollen to the fathomless, ancient gaze of the deep. Fingers wandering as she stared up at the moon, she cupped taut breasts and twisted pebbled nipples, gasping when a wave slapped her mound with a shock of cold.

"I am the chalice," she droned, shuddering at the way the

water trickled over heated flesh. Washing away the remnants of his possession—she felt it seep from her body with a liquid gush. A viscous testament to all that had been done to her. All that would be done. "My body the altar."

She was swollen. Aching with a need that surpassed mortal endurance.

But this was not surrender.

One hand tracing skin painted silver and blue, she framed her offer in prayer. Scant curves on full, lewd display. Legs splayed, knees parted as she found herself already slick and wanting. Her pussy heated, despite the chill of the ocean's kiss.

Sinking two fingers inside, she set the trap with the sweetest lure. Poisoned the surf with sacred feminine water and strummed that needy pearl exactly as he had done. Thumbing her clit, seeking relief from that relentless throb his venom had inspired.

"I am the chalice."

Above her, the stars shimmered in their celestial, endless dance. Indifferent to her plight, to the struggle raging within her.

"My body the altar."

Her fingers squelched. Twisted. Tormenting beaded flesh.

"My blood the sacrifice no god wants."

Heat bubbled through her skin, winding tighter as she worked.

"But you"—her breath hitched—"son of Poseidon... I feel you in my veins." Digging her heels in, she flexed, tipping her sex to meet the next crashing wave.

And so she didn't hear it when the water shifted.

She felt it.

A subtle change in the rhythm. The slap of cold seafoam lashed across her mound. And the rumble of something ancient rising from the deep. A song sung in her bones, it vibrated through every fiber of her being. Shook the sand beneath her until a solid went liquid and sucked her into a furious, possessive embrace.

Trapping her in place.

Her breath hitched, heart fluttering, but she persisted. Peeling gooey petals apart, she whispered, "I feel you in my marrow, beast. Staining my womb."

Abandoning her nipple, she reached to hold herself open with two hands. Showing him what he'd done to that sacred sheath.

"You are the tide," she said, back arching in the glove of sand when the sea splashed inside her. Cleansing her as the sand threatened to swallow her whole. But open, she remained. Inviting him to inspect what he'd defiled.

Nerves strung taut, teetering on the edge of a delirious fall, Kore spread her legs wider still. Her eyes fixed to the merciless glitter of indifferent stars above, her every spare ounce of attention ensnared by the ancient thing drifting closer. His impossible bulk shielding her from the crash of waves breaking and foaming across sleek, iridescent scales glimmering in her peripherals.

"And—" The final verse caught on a moan, before she whispered, "And I was meant to break across your cock."

His silent song fell quiet.

The sand held fast as the waves were directed away.

A shadow loomed above her, blotting out the stars. Replacing their luminous sheen with that which came from the deep.

Predatory eyes gleamed in the night as he looked upon the offering spread beneath him. Possessive. Feral. Snaking closer, his tail propelled him forward with an undulation that underscored just how big he truly was.

A leviathan of the deep.

Kore lay frozen beneath him. Aching for his touch—terrified to endure it.

Gills flapped above her. Exposing delicate filaments to the salty air. And with a curious tilt of his head, black hair clinging to his shoulders, a cruel smirk flickered at the edge of his lips.

It was a challenge.

A threat.

But she was a priestess. Consecrated, chosen by Apollo to worship the eternal flame—and she would not be extinguished so easily. Not even by the sea.

"I am the chalice," she said, enticing. Flirting with her doom. "So drink."

Teeth flashed in the night. A wicked grin gleaming white in the gloom, that shone with the confidence of a victory already secured.

She would be his tribute. Broken. Compliant. Obedient to the whims of a beast.

And so, she would forge a new power, one that lay between *female* legs.

Because she could take it. All he had to give.

Spread beneath him, pliant and welcoming, Kore watched the seam between man and leviathan bend back at a grotesque angle that defied human anatomy. Watched in muted awe as he lifted himself above her, poised to strike, so she might look upon him and see her end.

Her eyes caught on something that broke the pattern in iridescent scales.

It flexed. Bulging violently enough that the moon caressed what was hidden away, hinting at a monster concealed behind the protective sheen of scales.

Thrumming low in his throat, the beast huffed as his abdomen clenched—and his appendage broke through.

It wasn't a cock. Not in any mortal sense. It was a weapon. A serpent of flesh emerging wet and slick from the yawning divide in the armoured wall of scales. Glistening with a translucent sheen, it pulsed with want.

Sinister purpose.

Snaking free of his genital slit in morbid greeting, it was a dangerous, wicked thing. Inhumanly long. Thicker as it grew, widest at the base to support its own absurd weight, it reached for her. Almost… preening as she looked.

Pussy drooling into the wet sand, Kore couldn't so much as blink. Enthralled as ribs of flesh gleamed with that familiar glow, the very same blue pumping through her veins. His girth pulsed with beaded pearls bulging with every flex, before they sank back into the meat of his shaft, letting the skin smooth out, only to return with the next inhale of straining, flapping gills.

Breath frozen in her chest, Kore was struck silent. Horrified that such a thing had been inside her.

Mesmerized.

But her cunt gushed a sordid welcome. Warmth seeped from where she was empty. A slick fire simmering with desperate need.

She moaned.

Low and soft.

Followed by the flash of a pink tongue. Wetted lips, and a wanton whimper. Not a scream. Not a protest.

An invitation.

His slit bulged again when the base of that monstrous weapon strained toward her, and with an audible sound, his balls popped free. Massive, round. Each the size of her fist, they burst from his slit with a grotesque, wet slap against his scales, shimmering with the promise of what was boiling inside.

She met it head-on.

Staring directly at the thing he meant to cram back inside her.

"I am the chalice," she whispered and tried to tilt toward him where she was trapped in the sand. "You are the tide."

There was no denying this. No hiding from the inevitable.

Rumbling, the beast rewarded her compliance with another verse of that song beyond hearing. Gills fluttering, he took a breath that sounded wet. Painful. Shifting his massive coils until he'd claimed his place between her legs, scooped one massive hand behind her back and folded her up so she might watch while he worked.

His cock squirmed when he caught it around the middle, guiding it to the slick trench aching to be pummelled into submission. Saturating his tip in sweet human cream, nuzzling between puffy, swollen petals, he claimed her entrance.

Pausing long enough to catch her eye, letting his cock do its insidious work, he grinned.

And it was horrible.

With a hiss of effort, he penetrated her. Claiming that sodden sheath in a single, greedy thrust. Stretching her out, wider than anything she could have imagined, he remade her to suit his own whims and forced every drop of air from her lungs.

Splitting her asunder.

Kore tried to twist. Tried to scream or beg or whine.

Anything but the moan that bubbled forth.

But his gaze forced her honesty. Unblinking. Animal. Savage. He burrowed deep, a single relentless press that saw him batter the mouth of her womb as he bullied his way all the way inside.

She did *try* to resist.

Tried to be passive as she was wrenched wide open. Steeling herself against the wave of muscle barrelling inside, trying to pretend the stretch wasn't exquisite. That she didn't tilt her pelvis to get the bumps of his pearls to drag across her clit *just right*.

She tried...

... and failed.

And then he forced her to watch.

Directing her gaze down, he claimed a fist full of hair and made her bear witness to her defilement.

Lips gaping around a hollow, soundless scream, her eyes opened wide as glowing pearls bounced off her clit before they, too, were crammed into her cunt. Raking across the most sensitive part of her.

She watched that alien creature surge into her, stretching her pussy until it went bloodless and shone white in the silvery light of the moon. And through the skin below her navel, she could see it.

The glow.

Pearls twisting and tunneling.

She came, *hard.*

Climax crashed through her, and though her breath froze, and her hearing grew fuzzy and distorted, her skin came alive.

Her peak came unbidden, washing through her hard enough to drag her under. Clenching around that pulsing alien thing inside her.

There would be no shelter from this storm.

No escape for the thing she'd summoned.

There was only *this.*

Milking what squirmed between bloodless lips, she quaked. Thighs trembling, wrenched free of clinging sand, she tried to wrap her legs around his waist. To cling as dense muscle pounded against her, clamping down in a silly bid to slow the force of a tsunami crashing ashore.

Hopeless.

He dragged her inside out as he withdrew.

Wrenched a squalling orgasm from her body when he surged back inside.

Endless.

A scream was torn from her chest. A sob of pure, animal instinct that saw her resistance truly break.

Just as she'd asked.

Wet animal sounds of carnal fucking clapped on the beach.

Groans of two beasts in heat, joining for a purpose. Something vulgar. Ruled by instinct.

And then she felt it.

The anvil flare of his cock when it flattened out. Latching onto the mouth of her womb with ominous intent.

He paused, then. Buried to the hilt. Glued to the very end of her.

Long enough that she looked, left dangling at the edge of another glorious peak.

"Break me," she growled, her voice not her own. It was guttural and savage. "Give it to me, beast."

Fins flared in the moonlight. A start reminder of the creature rutting between her thighs. His inhuman nature.

And she watched when another wicked grin spread across his lips. When he showed her a spine hidden in a delicate fin. Letting his venom bead at the hollow tip, glowing blue in the night. And when he collected her hand in one large enough to crush her ribs, she didn't fight. Didn't pull away or thrash.

She watched.

Enthralled.

Stuffed.

Stretched.

He barbed her palm. Made her touch the tip and rewarded her with a shot of ecstasy. Rolling his hips as he dumped another load of venom into her veins, the beast fucked her raw. Savage.

And hips tilting back, Kore let him. Left herself open and locked her ankles higher around his waist. Setting an anchor as he pummelled her into the sand.

Absent shame.

Leaving streaks of red where she clawed at the massive chest heaving above her, her nails catching at the odd scale that speckled that broad, foreign skin.

Another violent peak seized her limbs, and she clenched around him. Convulsing, eyes rolling white. Trying to hold what no mortal could dare claim.

The sand beneath them grew clumpy with slick. Frothed by vigorous effort. Gushing free of gaping, ruined walls every time he pulled back—bubbling at her seams with every brutal invasion.

Kore sobbed as she clung. Cheeks wet with the grime of senseless tears. Throat raw with the moans forced from her chest.

" I-I am the ch-chalice," she stuttered, teeth clacking in time with snapping hips. "Y-Yours to break. To… to…"

Words failed her.

There was only this.

An alien, inhuman cock.

The pressure of it inside her, distorting her skin from the inside out. The shape of him moving within her, visible even in the dim light of deep night. And there, against that final gate guarding her womb… a blunt head seeking entrance.

Building to a height she'd never thought to jump from, Kore climbed. Her voice cracking on a moan as the pearls raked her clit and flung her into the abyss.

Pleasure swallowed her whole.

She came.

Violently.

Messy.

Vision flashing white as climax ripped her asunder.

Hips surging, the beast warbled deep in his chest and shifted. Wrapping one massive hand around her throat. Rough. Claiming her screams and silencing them, throttling the sounds even as he forced them from her ravaged voice box.

She felt it thicken, then. Catching at walls stretched to their limit, pressuring the lips of her poor, abused slit as she was made to gape around that flaring root. She felt the swelling at his base as he crammed it deeper, so the monster inside could feast.

With a guttural snarl, he came. Shuddering above her. Inside her. Gushing, a torrent of cum flooded her womb.

The sound was obscene as she wriggled on his hook. Caught. Limbs flailing as he pumped her belly full of sperm.

Eyes glassy, she sucked a breath between her teeth. Lifting her head to watch as her belly button danced. Pulsing with each gurgle of liquid dumped inside.

"Chalice," she slurred, and took every drop. Milking his shaft with clenching walls growing weaker with each passing moment. "I am... your... chalice... so..." Her eyes rolled back as another wave seized her limbs. "So..."

Time splintered as he bred her right there, in the dirt. Inflating her womb with buckets of ancient slime. Stretching her out and ruining her for any vague possibility that another male might one day enjoy her sacred cunt.

She woke when he snarled.

Wrenching himself free just as something bulbous had begun to bloom inside her. Catching the monster in one massive fist, he pumped himself empty. Sending lash after lash to paint her in his claim. It splattered her mound, matted in the fine tangle of hair, streaked the rounded curve of a swollen belly.

Dazed, she watched. Eyes bulging when he crushed a balloon of flesh at his base into submission and pumped the rest of his seed into the sand. A puddle of white left to pool between her cheeks.

Wasted.

The beast heaved for breath as he inspected his effort. A grin spread across full lips, despite the sweat beading his brow or the trickle of red escaping his gills.

And then he twisted, hefting one massive coil of his tail back to propel himself into the surf.

Alone.

Again.

Pussy gaping where he'd ruined her, she could feel thick sap oozing into the sand. Hot as spilled blood. Cooling in the night air as it went from syrup to gel. Thickening. Growing solid in his absence. Exposed to the air.

A sob chattered between her teeth. Ruined and weeping, her

thighs slick with shame, her slit spasming from horrible absence… she watched his tail vanish beneath the waves.

A blade in the moonlight.

"I am the chalice," she droned, and rolled to hands and knees. Eyes fixed to where she'd watched him vanish. "So… So… drink."

Her belly twisted with something she couldn't name.

Not hunger.

Not desire.

Need.

She crawled.

Ass upturned, gushing where she gaped, belly distended where it all but dragged through the sand.

Fingers trembling, Kore scooped a clot of cream into her palm.

Rescuing it from the sand.

And with a whimper, the vessel drank…

CHAPTER 15

*B*ubbles bled from his gills. Tiny fizzing things that tickled as he drifted through the current. Sinking, while he tried to simply draw breath through ravaged filaments. His every wound burning with the sting of brine.

Eyes that were meant for the dark had a disturbing white cast that lent a fog to everything he could see. His fins were blistered and oozing, sunburned and crisped from exposure, and his scales—once the envy of *Pelagorn* from the deepest trench to the warmest shallows—were curling. Peeling up at the edges.

He welcomed it.

The pain.

It was the price. Merely what he must endure in exchange for fucking his sun-kissed bride through her transformation. His divine flame. His obedient little whore, who spread those flimsy legs as wide as they might go and welcomed him inside. She'd commanded him to break her, the wild little thing.

Feckless, beautiful fool.

So eager to be his.

Kore Dionari.

His divine flame.

Perfect. A symbol of what he meant to do, the taboo he'd committed by taking a human from the sun, so he could drown her in the trench.

Her name rolled through his mind, making his cock throb, still swollen with the ghost of her scent. Echoing the moment she'd broken open around him.

Kore. Kore. Kore.

Soon.

It wouldn't be long before he could have her completely.

Black and endless, the trench yawned beneath him. A distant glow of bioluminescent blue calling to him from the deep. He sank, fins tattered and sailing as he folded in on himself, letting the pressure mend what the surface had ruined.

Blood heavy and thick, he snaked into the dark.

His passage disturbed the reef larvae still drifting through the trench—they clung to the tears in his scorched hide. Brushing against seared flesh and shredded scales.

A greeting from the Raskoril, his parasitical reef, they tasted his wounds. Cleaning away dead, flaking tissue. Feeding.

He thrummed, making the water tremble. Summoning the remaining larvae, he sent a purr rattling through his gills, letting the Resonance drum deep in his chest.

Shrouded in a cloud of ravenous larvae, Nyx sank through the heavy dark until the basin revealed itself. A bloom of soft light pulsing in the abyss.

In his absence, the reef had grown. Whole spires risen from volcanic vents of black heat. The entire basin breathed life into the deep.

An incredible feat, but one that could not sustain his bride. Not until the reef could produce enough oxygen-rich water to keep her alive, at so fragile a point in her transformation.

She was progressing rapidly, his Kore. Outpacing her predecessor by a degree he wouldn't have believed possible, if he hadn't felt the way she'd clenched and milked his cock. An exquisite mimic of a *Virelii* cunt, his little human was ravenous for everything he could cram inside.

It wasn't enough.

Not nearly enough to cradle the precious thing he'd drag into the dark.

Blue veins flickered through the dark. Fevered lightning, the Raskoril demanded tribute. Alive. Growing.

Hungry.

The reef was starving in the anoxic dark.

Settling on a shelf of barren rock, he brushed the feeding polyps off his scales and sent a handful sparkling into the dark. Watching the phantom of his fledgling kingdom shimmer and spread.

But he was too depleted, too injured to feed the reef, to force the growth at the same pace his bride had set.

He would heal. Rise again. Pay whatever the cost to keep her. Tame her.

The trench was quiet beyond the distant boom of tectonic heartbeats.

Still, except for the hum of the current endlessly pounding at the shore above.

And then the current shifted—subtle, at first. A scent he didn't recognize. One that didn't belong.

Nyx's spines rose.

Intruder.

Pelagorn.

He took a slow breath and tasted *Thalassari*.

Open-water scum.

Lip curling, Nyx scanned the trench with pupils blown wide and dared not move a muscle. Pain rippled beneath his scales anyway.

A scout.

One on a mission from the *Thalassari* king, no doubt. Drawn in by the scent of a Siren in the water, for it was a lure more potent than any other.

Forbidden.

His.

Glancing toward the distant basalt shelf where his trident stood embedded in the sea floor, Nyx hissed. Silent. Cursing himself for the blind stupidity of settling so far from that ancient forge of war.

Too far.

Too wounded.

Useless now, for a fight would finish what the surface had started.

And what would become of Kore, then? Half transformed. Abandoned.

Sensing his tension, the reef flashed a vibrant, hungry blue. Fragile tendrils stretched in the gentle current, microscopic maws gaping all around him.

Blind and searching for nutrition.

A shadow flicked through the dim light, trying to penetrate the fathomless dark.

The intruder.

A young male, inexperienced in the wars of kings.

Something sinister flicked over Nyxarion's face, then, and, sagging against the rock shelf, he feigned stillness. Watching the other circle, drifting in a cautious arc as he descended deeper into the cursed basin that shouldn't exist. Entranced by the glimmer of life in a place notorious for brutal absence.

The fledgling reef carpeted the sea floor.

Pulsing and glowing.

Impossible.

The scavenger neared. Close enough that Nyx could see the brilliant color of his scales and knew him to be *Thalassari*—of the warm, shallow seas and rich, easy living. Pretty and elegant, a creature of sunlit reaches. Ill-suited for the trench warfare he'd just floated into.

A halo of silver hair fell in silken waves over broad shoulders. Every unsure flick of his tail a fusion of opalescent silver and green. Color woven to catch the eye, and fins flared in a graceful spread. Wide and elegant, sailing on the sluggish current of toxic water.

Moving not to conquer, but to enchant.

Effortless seduction.

Eyes open wide to cling to every fragment of blue light, flicked with unease. Scanning the eternal black.

Nyx could taste his fear. More poisonous than the trench, it was a stink that singed his ravaged gills with a noxious fume.

Lips twisting, he watched the pretty fool gasp for every whisper of oxygen he could filter from the abyssal tide.

Waiting until he reached for a cluster of polyps that could be seen by even his weak *Thalassari* eyes.

Ravenous filaments uncoiled, brushing outstretched claws. Light flashed in the gloom, as if in greeting.

"Beautiful, isn't it?" Nyx hummed, making the other *Pelagorn* whirl with a hiss of exposed spines. "You've come far from home, *Thalassari*. These are... dangerous waters."

The intruder ejected a plume of violet venom, emptying his venom sacs. "This—what you've done—it's an abomination!"

Nyxarion laughed, tail flicking through the dense current. "This is progress, boy. This is survival."

"This is—you can't do this! No human brood are to be seeded after the Accord of Nisyros. Your own father stripped you of title for breaking the Accord. For risking Thalos' wrath with your repulsive crimes. And you dare to—"

"Dare?" Nyx hummed, unable to stop his spines from twitching. "This is the Black Sea, boy. I conquered it. Fed it. Your every breath here is a gift of my making. I dare *nothing*. Because here, my whim is law."

"Thalos—"

A vicious snarl erupted from between Nyx's clenched teeth. "The open-water king has no dominion here."

But the interloper would not be deterred. "I followed her scent! It's in the current. Her perfume reaches all the way to the Dardanelles. It fouls the Bosphorus with the truth of what you've done here, Nyxarion Korrides. If Thalos hasn't scented her yet, he *will*. It will ride the next tide. Undeniable."

Tattered scales lifting to vent the heat of his fury, Nyx said nothing. Choosing silence as the interloper drifted closer in all his righteous fury… closer as ravenous tendrils unfolded with delicate grace that his weak, *Thalassari* eyes couldn't see.

"Look at you," the intruder continued, oblivious, gesturing at Nyx, where he was coiled on the shelf. "Haggard. Scales flaking away with the tide. Sunburned. Pathetic the way only an *Abyssari* can manage," he sneered, fins flicking a delicate dance. "Fucking trench-born. Can't handle the surface. You were born for the dark, but still, you dare to take another bride after your abysmal failure with the first?" A sharp bark of laughter sliced through the dark, and his spines ejected another spurt of violet venom. Bright and beautiful and deadly. "Thalos marked your name, exile. He'll come, just as I did. Drawn in by the putrid scent of your whore. And then he'll tear this place apart."

Not bothering himself to move, Nyx tilted his head. Watching as the interloper drifted much, much too close. "Is that so?"

"An example will be made," he blathered on. "Her bones shall be used for decoration in the gleaming halls of Caelith Mare. Her flesh peeled to feed the tides as a reminder for all that the Accord of Nisyros is what allows you revolting detritus-eaters to continue on—at Thalos' pleasure."

The reef flared a warning too subtle for *Thalassari* eyes to perceive, reacting to the wrath festering in Nyx's veins. "She is mine," he crooned, letting his voice carry the full weight of his station. "From her, I will reclaim what was stolen, and your pathetic accord will rot in tides that will remember a new sovereign."

Grinning, Nyx flicked his spines and silently commanded the reef to strike without moving so much as a fin in the interloper's direction.

Tiny filaments latched to pretty, glittering scales. Gentle at first, too soft for the other male to notice.

"Thalos will hear of this," the interloper promised, unaware his song had already ended in horror. "You have hours, exile. Thalos will turn this trench to silt before you can breed her."

Nyx's grin only grew, for without any effort at all, the filaments pierced scale and muscle, dragging the other *Pelagorn* down with a startled shriek that bubbled as it left his doomed lips.

"Oh, she's already been bred, *Thalassari*," he hummed, shifting to slither from the shelf. Swimming closer to watch the struggle of his parasitic reef when it sent thousands of tiny barbs into muscle. Siphoning what it wanted from the struggling male's blood and bone. "She progresses fast enough that even I, First Sovereign King of the Black Sea, struggle to prepare for my bride to drown. But here you are," he said, and laughed when the other thrashed and struggled even as his flesh was sloughed from bone. "Bringing gifts for my coronation. An example will be made," he mocked. "Your bones shall be used to tether my bride at my side. In death, you shall keep her open and ready for my knot. Your scales saved for decoration that will be used to please my bride as she is bred before my court."

"Vile fucking—" He tried to scream, but the sound rose as a wall of bubbles. Fragile and cut short, for the Raskoril encircled the interloper's throat in a milky curl that sent blood misting through the black. Polyps glowing an excited, violent blue, they claimed the *Thalassari* song as tribute.

Nyx thrummed, letting the Resonance rattle as the other's

body was stretched taut. Purring as he watched joints burst and viscera spill in garish ribbons of fetid gore.

Lingering, savoring the display as his fledgling reef swelled against the bedrock. Each crunch echoed his savage pleasure as his unspoken whim was obeyed.

And in return, the Raskoril feasted.

Flesh melted to pale jelly.

Blood siphoned into the heart of hardening coral.

Until there was nothing left but scale and bone. Gleaming white. A cage clutched in coral fist.

"Perfection," Nyx hummed, brushing a finger along one of the ivory ribs. "You'll be given true purpose."

Satiated, the Raskoril quieted. Its glow dimmed as it worked to digest the prize it had been given.

Nyxarion inspected the bone lattice—the curve of the spine, the robust cage of ribs—and saw her within it. Thrashing against her inevitable surrender, perhaps. But kept safe. Hidden from what would come.

He knew it now.

Thalos.

The open-water king.

Time was running out.

And this would be her cradle.

Her throne.

Lingering a moment as exhaustion spread through his limbs, he pressed a hand to the surface and commanded the Raskoril to obey, letting it taste his intention through his blood. "For you," his voice rippled. "So no false king may touch what is already mine."

CHAPTER 16

The sun woke her.

Pitiless heat. Merciless and cruel, it beat down upon her face where she lay sprawled on the beach, baking her into a crust of sand and dried fluids. Thigh throbbing where she'd been barbed with yet another dose of venom.

Kore groaned. Her voice a soundless, hollow rasp. And, sucking a breath through chapped and flaking lips, she cringed back from the harsh glare. Pulling her left arm from where it was glued to the beach, she tried to shield her eyes from the searing pain.

But her skin… it was caked in a thick layer of sand. Itchy and tight. Stiff and clumpy.

The flash of clenched knuckles flicked through her memory, and she remembered the ropes of burning white. The obscene sounds he'd made as he'd sprayed his mark across her skin… as she'd cupped that cooling seed in trembling hands and…

It clung to her thighs, her belly… her breasts—everywhere the ropes of burning hot seed had coated her. Everywhere the monster's cum had gone from cream to pearly gel was now dried in a thick, clinging layer that refused to crumble or flake.

Groaning, sore from nipples to toenails, she tried to brush it off and found it stubborn enough to pull at her skin.

A stark reminder of what she'd done. How far she'd fallen.

She couldn't bring herself to look.

No, the weight of her belly alone was enough.

Skin stretched taut, a grotesque mockery of middle pregnancy, she was swollen with shame. Bloated with monster cum. On full, lewd display where she'd been left in a puddle of cooling fluids on the beach. Exposed.

But there was no one to see her shame.

Only the harsh, unforgiving glare of the sun that never blinked.

Trying to roll, Kore twisted—and her belly shifted with her. Sloshing heat sealed inside her womb. Not a child, not a gluttonous meal… but the leavings of a leviathan too large for her body to contain.

Panting, she struggled to her hands and knees and let the sun scowl at her back. Sweat beading along her brow, she clenched her molars and hissed, "Get up. Now."

There was work to be done.

Time to mark.

With a huff, she staggered to her feet—and fell. Wobbling with the change in her center of gravity, thrown off balance. Limbs shaking, her knees buckled.

The sun glowered at her back, mocking her effort.

Squinting against the brilliant glare, she clenched her eyes shut against that once-beloved golden radiance and shielded her face. Breath coming slow and thick.

Laboured.

Lungs squashed against the colossal weight pressing against her diaphragm, straining to draw a breath that wasn't dry and thin, Kore gagged. Retching at the reek of rot bubbling in the heat, plagued by the memory of what she'd done.

That she could still taste him.

Still smell the brine.

Nothing but bile came up. Stringy and yellow, for her belly was empty. Gone was the desperation of yesterday. The need to fill her belly with something, *anything* that might wash the venom away.

Now, there was only him.

The bitter tang of salt. Sweet with the memory of the sea.

She lifted her head. Blinking glassy eyes at the glittering expanse sprawling out before her.

Was he there? Watching?

Lurking beneath the surface, biding his time.

Blood boiling with pure spite and self-loathing, she piled rocks atop the place she'd woken up—where the tide waters had been for his last visit. Marking an atoll in the sand, just so she could be ready to mark the next.

And the next.

Sweating freely in the heat, skin pale and blistered, she turned. One trembling hand raised to block the sun from her eyes, she waddled back. Away from the sea and all her dark promises. Away from the stabbing betrayal sending golden light slicing through her skull.

She fled.

Fast as she could.

Belly swollen, pendulous and shifting with every unsteady step, Kore wobbled back to the cave.

Her gait hesitant and wrong. Feet dragging in the sand, clumsy and unstable, she slogged toward the promise of shelter in the dark. Dodging slippery rocks wet with algae, shallow tide pools, and clumps of reeking beach rot, her ribs straining under the weight in her gut.

And when she was shielded in the gloom, hidden from the painful bite of searing heat, Kore allowed her gaze to stray. Inspecting her palm. The spot where a new barb had penetrated her flesh, where veins of toxic blue spidered out from a fresh wound.

Venom.

He was inside her, even now.

Lingering.

Blinking in the half-light, she stared at her feet. Seeing what *wasn't* there.

Bruises.

Cuts and scrapes.

There should have been signs of the battle he'd waged upon her body. Evidence that she'd been fucked raw. Ravaged by scale and claw and greedy, ravenous appetite for every scrap of female flesh.

But there was only this.

A swollen belly, clumps of clinging sand glued to her skin, and a tiny wound pulsing blue.

It wasn't natural, how quickly she'd healed.

But then… was there anything natural about drowning in the Aegean Sea, only to be crushed beneath an Athenian trireme, revived by a son of Poseidon, and remade as his chalice?

A humorless laugh bubbled between chapped lips.

She remembered it in flashes. The pulse of him grinding inside her. His girth swelling, stretching her rim when he'd climaxed, pumping an impossible pressure into her womb. The splash of seed when he tore himself free with an inhuman roar…

She was covered in it.

Itchy with sand and clotted cream.

It had hardened while she lay unconscious on the beach. A cast of itching shame she couldn't simply brush away.

Because she was unclean.

Filthy.

A monster's whore.

She staggered to her feet with a single, desperate thought screaming in her mind.

Clean.

She had to get clean.

Even if it meant braving the sea to do it. Even if she had to endure the scornful, unblinking gaze of the sun, she would wash herself clean of the monster's sperm.

Splashing into the shallows, she collapsed in the surf with a hiccuping sob. Eyes leaking painful tears as the light stabbed into her skull.

The sea greeted her with a cool embrace, lapping gently at sensitive skin.

Stooping, Kore splashed her face. Scooped water over her arms and chest. Scrubbing every inch she could reach.

Still, the sand clung.

Falling away in stubborn clumps.

Wading just a little deeper, shins wet with lapping waves, she kept her eyes fixed to any hint of what lay beneath the surface, and bent to work.

"Come on," she hissed, clawing at the grime. Scrubbing until her skin was raw and unblemished. Pristine, despite what she'd endured beneath the bulk of a colossus rutting above her.

Hands flashing, Kore scooped water over her belly. Her thighs.

And then, taking a steadying breath, she splashed that cool relief between her legs. Too afraid to touch what was swollen, not with abuse...

... but need.

Teeth flashing white, she abandoned her cleft and scrubbed her belly. Ignoring everything but the drive to be scoured clean. Her nails turned to claws, leaving streaks of raised flesh where his grip had been cruelest—where her hip met the crease of her thigh, and seed had pooled when he'd finished defiling her.

There was grit there, too.

Scowling, Kore scratched at the filth until her fingernail caught at something sharp.

Something embedded in her skin.

She yelped. Cursing as her lip curled, she pinched the speck between thumb and forefinger and pulled. Prying it loose with a sharp pang and a hiss of held breath.

Sharp. Tiny and thin.

She frowned against the blinding light, trying to see through eyes that couldn't bear the light.

"A shell?" she murmured, squinting at the fragment caught between her fingers. A bit of flotsam driven into her skin by his weight. His merciless, punishing thrusts.

Prodding it, turning it in her palm, Kore's brow grew furrowed at the razor edges and pretty shimmer.

It wasn't a shell.

Her breath hitched as the glitter of iridescent color slithered through her memory. Color scattering and sparkling across the cave walls, sliding together with a smooth glide as he'd moved to mount her.

A scale.

He'd fucked her hard enough to leave a scale embedded in her thigh.

Staggering back, collapsing into wet sand, Kore twisted so she might inspect the tiny wound it had left behind. Peering down at the tendril of crimson trailing down her leg.

The sun pounded against her back.

Eyes throbbing in their sockets, a headache flared inside her skull with every blink, making her foggy and slow.

How long did she have before the beast returned? Before the tide rolled in and brought another wave of abuse and pleasure?

Absent-minded, she scratched at the itch nagging at her wrist.

Would he take her throat again? Occupy himself with the treacherous seam between her legs? Or... invent some new horror to visit upon her?

With a shudder, Kore blinked. Itching until a flicker of pain tore her gaze from the sea.

She frowned at the spot.

Letting the pad of her fingers drift over the sharp edge, her brows drawn tight. Vision blurred and warped by the white-hot ache pulsing behind her eyes.

But even through the blistering pain of a blooming migraine, she knew.

Half sunken into her skin, the razor edge of a tiny fan flashed in the sunlight.

Prying it loose, Kore tore it free. Hardly bothering to hiss at the sting, ignoring the bead of blood welling in the wound, she smeared the tiny thing across the heel of her palm.

Pretty.

Soft gold at the center, fading to an ember-orange, with pink edges. Shot through with streaks of rose. A sunset.

Beautiful.

Delicate.

Feminine.

Lip curling, Kore flicked it into the surf.

She didn't see where it landed before the sea took it. Gulping it down. Greedy and immediate. There and gone before she might look again.

It was bad enough that he'd fucked her hard enough to leave her swollen and raw, but to leave pieces of himself lodged in her skin?

"Animal," she hissed, and ignored the way her cunt flexed, her belly growing hard as her muscles pined for more. Choosing instead to watch the spot where the scale had vanished beneath the waves.

Blood trickled down her wrist, then. A thin, jagged trail veined red against the sand and surf. She stared at the spot, watching it ooze until it... stopped. Until the flesh knit before her eyes.

Her heart skipped.

Because it wasn't possible.

Turning her bleary gaze away—a denial—she spotted a clam nestled in the sand and seized the distraction.

Lumbering forward, she stepped deeper into the surf. Chilled and sobering, the water licked at her thighs. Cooling what the sun had baked and burned.

She stooped, groaning as she moved around her own obscene girth.

Shaking, she went to her knees with a hiss, reaching for the clam…

… and froze.

Her skin caught Apollo's divine light.

The migraine throbbed between her temples. A rainbow blur through the pain.

But she saw it.

A web of iridescence tracing her forearm. Smooth beneath the skin. Too precise, too perfect… because it was a pattern.

Scales.

Tiny and translucent, layered. An armored filigree written beneath the surface.

Not shining with the greens and purples of the beast.

These were…

A sunrise.

Pale gold, blooming into pink. Bleeding into baby coral.

"No," she whispered, breath catching high at the back of her throat. She sat back on her heels, horrified. "No, no, no…"

She reached for the trailing edge. Tracing the razor-sharp fan of the last scale until it slipped through to the surface, sailing on a bead of crimson.

A thread of pain lanced through her nerves, but she pressed harder. Letting her nail slip beneath it, freeing it enough to tug.

The skin tented where it was attached.

Attached.

With a hitching breath, Kore tore it free and watched the

blood well from the wound. Watched the bead burst free and trickle down her forearm.

The trail wasn't smooth.

It was jagged…

… around more.

Raised bumps lurking beneath the surface. A lattice, dozens of them lying flush and uniform. Following the natural lines of tendons and bone. Arranged in a perfect geometry too neat to be the result of chaotic fucking.

A whisper escaped her lips, and with a breathy, repeated, "No, no, *nooo*," she began to scrub anew. Fists full of sand, scouring her own skin, she scrubbed. Efforts redoubled, fueled by panic and denial, until she was chafed and raw from the elbows down. Rubbing hard enough to leave ribbons of red etched into her skin.

It didn't work.

Because the scales weren't foreign bodies embedded by vigorous rutting.

They weren't morbid souvenirs won beneath the pummelling weight of a demi-god.

They were hers.

A tight, spiraling pattern scrawled across the backs of her fingers, curled over the ridge of her wrist. Trailing in a shimmering arc from elbow to bicep and beyond. Tiny, translucent plates—each shining with the shades of a stunning sunrise—speckled her body.

Itching where they promised to break through into the light.

The more she scrubbed, the more obvious they became. Shining against the reddened, angry shade of flushed skin.

A pattern.

Hers.

Screaming, giving life to the panic bubbling in her chest, Kore scrambled back from the poisonous lure of cool waters and quiet, lapping waves. Breath choppy. Belly distended and sloshing, her balance betrayed her, sending her crashing into the beach.

The sun caught the glimmer of emerging scales and forced her to look.

Below the surface, more color. Tiny speckles curled around her nipples, delicate fans spiraling across her sternum in dainty patterns. Ridges of skin glossed with pressure pressing up from below.

Her fingers brushed lower, then. Tracing the swell of her enormous belly. Where she'd been inflated and marked.

More scales. Bigger ones, making the skin of her outer hips rough. Textured. A clear trail she couldn't help but follow.

Cautious, her fingers wandered in. Tracing the curve of her thigh, she touched what had once been given in service to the divine. The skin there had always been soft. Sacred. A place marked for the gods and priests who served them.

Now?

She moaned, and it was a fragile, terrified thing.

What she found was tight.

Slick.

And the soft brush of downy hair?

It sloughed off in clumps that clung to her fingers, in its place… something sharp.

Smooth and hard.

Tiny ridges where there should have been nothing but the divine feminine.

A sob chattered through her teeth.

She shouldn't have touched herself.

Shouldn't have given in to the morbid curiosity.

But she had to know.

"Nooo," she moaned, hand clapping over her mouth to stifle a scream. Sinking her teeth into the meat of her thumb, Kore drew blood. Disrupted the lacy pattern that shouldn't exist.

The sun vanished behind a cloud.

But the sea crept higher. Crashing against the shore, swirling around her thighs. And in a surge that was almost a caress, it washed over her hips. Seeping inside her to touch what had been desecrated by a monster.

Something inside responded.

At the touch of the sea, the seal inside her burst.

There was no warning.

Only a flood of sperm returning to the element it had been born of.

A strangled screech gurgled from her chest, and Kore convulsed. Eyes wide before they rolled white, belly flexing as a torrent of thick, pearlescent seed spilled out of her.

Climax roared through her with the force of a rogue wave. Her limbs flailing in the shallow water, pussy clenching in waves as a river rushed between her legs.

Panting, she lay in the shallows, dazed. Sightless gaze staring up at a looming storm cloud that offered blessed relief from the blinding morning light. Belly no longer swollen, pussy throbbing with aftershocks of the tectonic event that had just moved through her. Her heart pulsing beneath the corners of her jaw.

It wasn't the horror of it.

The obscene thrill of being emptied.

It was the knowing.

Of what she'd just done. That he'd catch the scent of in the water...

... and return with the tide to put it back...

CHAPTER 17

Gills fluttering, Nyx hung suspended in the crushing embrace of the deep. Eyes closed. Brow furrowed. Cradled in the frigid dark at the bottom of the trench, he reveled in the balm of his element.

Soothed by the pressure.

Made whole by the depths he'd been born to rule.

Alone.

Recovery was slower this time. His lungs labouring, even now.

Cracking one eye, he watched the current take a handful of scales and scatter them across the sea floor.

There was a toll.

A price.

One he was willing to pay to claim his prize, *yes*, but expensive nevertheless.

The effort to breed her had flayed him, savaging sensitive skin, strip by agonizing strip. His every heaving breath acidic, every glint of the sun a flensing blade that had left him ragged and raw.

Lungs meant to sieve oxygen from brine sizzled with the

surface's wretched poison. Scales designed to protect sensitive skin were scorched by the sun, dried out, and flaking off his hide in great, glittering sheets.

He coughed, a convulsion of muted agony. Lungs still dry, despite his return to the trench. Blood—thick and dark—spiraled from his gills in a lazy plume that curled in the current. Twisting before his eyes as the trench stitched him back together in silent judgment.

This was the cost of feeding Kore in a world that hated his kind. A world that punished those who refused to bend.

Thalos' world.

He spat, watching another dark ribbon unspool. Trying to soak in the chill.

To heal.

It wasn't working.

He wasn't recovering fast enough—he could feel it. The brutal, crushing weight of being on land lingered even when he'd returned to the clenched fist of the trench. And the gaps between breeding his delicious little captive and recovery only grew. Yawning wider as a warning knell sounded in the deep.

The *Thalassri* King was coming.

His vision blurred. Bones aching, skin burning.

This pace…

It wasn't sustainable.

At this rate, he'd die before he might see what she'd become. Before Thalos arrived with his legion of *Thalassari* to quell this fledgling rebellion.

Nyx glanced up, squinting through the pain throbbing behind his eyes. Up, toward the distant twinkle mocking him from above.

He'd have to push her harder.

That soft, breakable thing.

What had she called herself?

His chalice.

Grinning now, Nyx's fins flared when the current tried to lift him. Holding him in place despite the force trying to move him. One hand darting out to seize his trident, his cock flexed behind his slit.

It was the memory.

That tiny, human cunt. So much less responsive than a *Virelii*. But it was the way he didn't quite fit. The way she'd gripped him, milking his shaft for every drop of cum. Begging with words and slick. Belly inflating with his seed. And when her legs had locked around his waist? When she'd screamed and bucked and begged?

He'd forgotten the agony of his task.

The looming pressure of time running short.

Forgot everything except the silken grip of a slit redesigned just for him.

One he'd remake, so she could take more.

Oh, yes. He'd push his little human. Harder. *Faster*. Forcing his venom into her, corrupting her until he washed away her revolting humanity and forced the bloom that had gotten him exiled. Cast out. Punished for daring to claim what no other could fathom.

It was taboo to take a human and give it to the sea. Something the *Thalassari* courts had outlawed before he'd even been spawned.

He spat into the black waters.

The Accord of Nisyros.

It had cost him the throne, never mind that his people—the *Abyssari*—were inching ever closer to extinction. That the restrictions imposed upon them by the *Thalassari* king were going to kill them all.

Lip curled, Nyx flicked his tail.

Cowards.

Too afraid of the Thalos to venture even the tip of a fin out of line. Even if it meant their doom.

Planting his trident into the seabed once more, Nyx sent a

cloud of silt billowing into the current. The triple-pronged tips gleamed with ominous intent.

He would not submit.

Not to *Pelagorn* law.

Not to open-water kings, or the laws of the trench-born.

Not to *her*.

This was the Black Sea, and here, Nyx was law.

The trident pulsed. Unused since his exile, hungry for battle, eager to serve. A weapon only the *Abyssari*-born king might handle.

Around him, the trench responded.

Sluggish, at first.

Quiet.

But alive. As if waking from a long sleep after a gluttonous feed.

The sand shifted, silt dancing against the current to reveal the bedrock. A canvas on which he would paint his *second* greatest creation.

Establishing what was to be his seat of power.

In defiance of Caelith Mare, where Thalos ruled, and in solemn tribute to his ancestral home, Threnakar, where his father was content to wither.

This was to be a new court, one not of the deep nor the shallows.

Vorynthar.

The name rang with the clear trill of truth.

A heretical reef born of Raskoril Coral. Fed from his own blood, his venom... and, of course, whatever hapless fools dared to drift too close.

Nyx grinned, pleased with the progress of the colony that bore his mark. Tending to every barbed, bony finger that lifted in greeting with a wave of semi-sentient reverence.

He dragged his palm across the trident's obsidian tips.

The pain was crisp. Clean. Ritualistic.

Before the current could erase it, he pressed his wound to the tiny polyps.

The coral drank.

Tiny mouths gnawed at the iron-rich feast offered.

It grew.

Faster than it should have, twitching before fanged spirals curled out from bone-white sockets. Barbed and coiled, growing in time with his pulse.

He watched it bloom around the bones of Thalos' sentry.

Not a throne.

Not a nursery.

It was to be a vault.

One meant to contain a treasure.

The ghost of the shape flickered in the deep, pulled straight from the sinister corners of his imagination, built on a *Thalassari* skeleton. Knitting itself along a bony frame, invisible even to his keen gaze.

Ribs of hollow bone flickered in the dark.

He smiled.

And the coral drank.

Soon.

Soon, the sound of her panting would echo through the depths. Her cunt clenching, milking him dry as her body begged for more.

And he would give it to her.

Knot her before the eyes of the court.

Claim her for the Black Sea and start a new era.

His cock burst from his vent, swollen and eager. Remembering her defiance. Her pleas and tears.

The perfect little whore was the first brick in the foundation of his fledgling kingdom. One that Thalos could never simply take, for it was to be built on a bride who would break only for him.

"You are the tide."

Showing teeth, Nyx flicked his tail and brought one of his spines forward. Stabbing the eldest polyp at its base, and letting it drink the toxin Kore would need to complete her transformation from grotesque to regal.

Consumed by his task. Giving everything he could spare.

The pain was exquisite.

Lancing through his body in ripples, sharp and cleansing as the venom gland pulsed and emptied. Beneath him, the reef shivered. Hungry larvae flexing as if swallowing his toxin deep into their lattice.

Barbs flared. Thin spirals grew calcified and thick. The whole structure throbbing in tandem with his heart, glowing with a luminous blue light as unnatural veins grew tuberous and sluggish with his essence.

Back arching, his gills flared wide. Scales fanning out to vent the heat of his effort. He would bleed for his kingdom the way Thalos would never understand, sacrificing his own health in the privacy of the treacherous Black Sea. A place so hostile, none of the *Pelagorn* had ever dared to colonize it.

But he would.

Already, his reef was filtering the basin's anoxic, poisonous layers, making it rich with oxygen. Fertile with all the ingredients needed for his bride to thrive in the harshest possible clime.

Breath coming short and hard, Nyx reached for the next fragment—and froze.

The current shifted.

Hardly perceptible.

But laced with something familiar.

That scent.

It rippled through his gills.

Filled his lungs.

His own seed laced the current.

Drifting.

Diluted by the sea.

Tainted with the sweet nectar of the bride he cultivated.

"Defiant slut," he snarled, low and vicious. Fear pulsing through his veins, he tore his hand away from the reef and dislodged his barb with a howl so black, the ancient kings would shiver and cringe.

That scent in the water could only mean one thing.

She had gone into the surf.

Long enough for the plug he'd crammed inside her to dissolve and send a torrent of sperm gushing into the water.

She was trying to escape.

Or worse.

She'd been found.

Spines flaring, lips peeled back in a soundless snarl, for it was too soon to return, his body nowhere near recovered from the effort he'd expended to fill her womb.

Pain lanced through his system when he whirled.

He ignored it.

Kore was fleeing or taken, and he would not lose another bride.

Gills burning, skin tender and raw, he snarled—at his back, the Raskoril hissed. Reactive to the surge in his pulse, it spat a plume of bubbles from tiny chambers, as if recoiling from his vicious temper.

A low groan rumbled through the trench, and with war in his heart, Nyxarion Korrides, first Sovgerine of the Black Sea, reached for the trident.

Thalos would not have her.

It thrummed the moment his fingers touched ancient metal. Obsidian-dark, the shaft grew resonant with the hum of power it hadn't tasted in years.

Not since he'd failed.

Exiled from the kingdom he should have ruled.

The trident remembered war.

He wrenched it from where it had been embedded in the sediment with a howl of rage. Tail thrashing off the bottom, he launched himself toward the surface. Eyes gone black and fathomless in an instant as he made the ascent at a speed that would kill any other creature in the ocean.

But he was no longer a king.

No longer a builder of something profound and new.

He was a monster ascending.

A predator on the hunt, seething with the need to punish and claim. Drunk with a surge of possessive violence and territorial hunger, he shot through the poisonous layers. A bolt through the dark. Carrying enough speed to leave a trail of scales glittering in his wake.

Every stroke of his tail dragged fire through his chest. Left his gills burning and raw. His lungs squeezed tight as he abandoned the snug embrace of the deep and returned once more to her domain.

The surface.

Pulsing in his grip, the trident thrummed with an ancient power. Ready to enact the frothing wrath festering in his heart.

Ready for war.

He didn't just want her swollen and full, oh no. This time, he'd see her ruined with it.

He'd either rut her over the broken corpse of his enemies or punish her for daring to flee.

Vibrating in his grip, the trident shimmered, eager for battle. Humming with the thirst for carnage. To pin her to the beach and make her learn exactly who she belonged to.

He burst from the surf with a snarl.

Eyes scanning the brilliant, radiant sunlit beach for traitors.

White-hot agony lanced through his lungs, but he didn't slow. The sun blindingly hot overhead, salting the flayed strips of scales peeling from his flesh.

None of it mattered.

She had gone into the surf. Dared to flee.

And he would make her pay.

Trident gripped tight, the shaft bit his palm, and drank his fury. Feasting on the rage. Luxuriating in the tempest boiling his blood.

The beach shimmered ahead.

Utterly absent any hint of *Pelagorn*—*Thalassari* or *Abyssari*.

So she'd tried to flee, then.

He grinned, and it was terrible.

Propelling himself from the surf, Nyx slithered. Planting the trident into the beach, carving deep gouges in the stone of unseen bedrock, he moved. Labourious. Determined. Ignoring the blistered skin, the flaking scales. The coppery tang of blood from gills straining to draw enough oxygen into his lungs.

He was a storm.

Something possessed.

Gills clattering with effort, he inhaled the blistering air. A thunderous scowl marred his brow. Eyes gone dark as pitch scanned the beach for his wayward prize and found her absent.

Wrath, pure and unfiltered, threatened to consume him, for she wasn't in the surf. Not sprawled out on the beach.

She was gone.

For a moment, panic threatened to eclipse his temper. That she would dare. Risk herself to scorn his gift.

But a tangle of darkness caught his blackened gaze.

The cave.

The place where he'd fuck her into the stone until she learned what it was to belong to the sea.

Hefting his tail, snaking up the beach without the tide to ease his passage, Nyx used the ancient weapon as a crutch and not the god-killer it was meant to be. A trail of tattered scales left glittering in his wake, gills hissing with every laboured breath he dragged into soggy lungs.

She was there.

Curled in the back of the cave, as far from the sunlight as she could get. Sleeping. Hands cradling a flat belly. A tiny shadow wrapped around the center of what had once been a human girl.

And her skin…

… it was glowing.

His vision—meant for the endless black of abyssal things— caught the shimmer in an instant. Bioluminescent scribbles pulsed beneath her skin. A dainty webbing scrawled across her throat, spirals painted over her collarbones. Elegant swirls snaking up her arms, where her veins pulsed with the heart of the sea.

A flush of desperate want rolled through him, slaking his lust for war with a wave of need.

The transformation had taken root.

His cock stirred, twitching with primal instinct. Obsessive, carnal want of a thing he had no business craving but couldn't ignore.

He should have waited—the flaking scales and misted blood clouding his every breath was proof enough of that. That his body was failing. Gills shredded, lungs spitting fire, blood filled with bubbles and too thin to endure the punishment of the surface for much longer.

But there she was.

Empty, waiting to be filled.

His human chalice.

His Siren bride.

The trident hummed in his grip. Whispering dark promises. Punishment and violence, an offer to claim her. Cage her. Mark his little human in a way she hadn't yet imagined possible. Its pull was ancient, a relic of kings and tyrants.

Enticed, he dragged himself forward. One arm at a time. Bulk bunching and shifting behind him, as the thump of the trident crashed into stone.

When he reached her, he paused.

Just long enough to breathe.

To watch.

Memorize the light blooming beneath her skin, and *know*.

She could run.

But she could never leave.

Nyx let his fingers slide down the trident's shaft, releasing the insidious power. Abandoning the trident where it was embedded in the stone.

And then he threw all caution to the poisonous wind…

… and reached for his bride.

CHAPTER 18

*S*he was clean.

Consecrated.

Unbroken by the cruelty of men.

"The Oracle commands you to give," the high priest murmured in a voice that echoed and shivered, licking thin lips. Watery eyes watching her from beneath a heavy hood. *"Your lord Apollo commands you to break."*

Bowing her head, heart in her throat, Kore nodded. Letting spotted, aged hands push the robes from her shoulders to reveal the nudity hidden beneath scratchy wool. He guided her back, spreading her across the altar where he would spill vestal blood to bless the Spartan army.

Kore submitted as she was trained to do. Watching dust motes spin through shafts of sunlight, painting Apollo's inner sanctum in brilliant golds and deepest purples, she lay beneath a doughy weight and trembling forearms. Staring up at the high vault in the heart of the temple. The stone cool beneath naked flesh, her shoulder blades cutting into the unforgiving granite, her nose stinging with the scent of charred rosemary and sage.

She was warm. Floating.

Unable to feel the priest's probing fingers, his frantic thrusts, for his paltry efforts were eclipsed. Drowned out by the monstrous ache already pulsing inside her.

Demanding every wayward drop of attention she might spare.

The sunbeam narrowed, growing sharp and cruel. Slicing at her skin with treacherous, savage heat. Burning what it touched—her arms and face, shoulders and spine—forcing her to cower away from Apollo's unforgiving glare.

She hissed at the pain and turned to the dark. To the cool embrace of the deep.

She was pulled under.

Forced to the crushing depths, beneath the impossible weight of an Athenian trireme. Pinned to the sea floor, her lungs filled with the sea, while her belly was filled to bursting with brine...

She woke with a gasp and found herself pinned, face pressed to stone.

Not crushed beneath the shattered hull of a warship, this was not the weight of wood or wreckage.

It was flesh.

Slick. Scaled. Achingly familiar. Pussy already wrenched wide open, she'd been stuffed with a pressure she'd come to know. One that swelled from inside. One she craved.

He was back.

Fucking her into the stone with the sort of desperate savagery she'd never known possible before she'd drowned. Rutting into her from behind, his weight a burden on her slender body as he worked her tight sheath and forced it to accept all that was inhuman and vicious.

There was a fury in his grip. His thrusts brutal and erratic. Not the calculated rhythm of the divine creature with intelligent designs upon her flesh, but the animalistic beat of a mindless rut. Something wild. Punishing and cruel.

Fingers clawing at his belly, she cried out as he pummelled her from above.

"Pl-please!" she moaned into the stone, stuttering and breathless as his cock shoved inside her. Crushing her lungs with each heavy thrust. "What have I done?"

His answer was a wet, wordless snarl. Cruel fingers tipped her hips up until her back was made to arch, and desperate hands braced against the wet cave floor were the only thing stopping her from being folded in half. Until she was wide open for his vicious attention and he was sheathed so deep inside her, she could feel her belly tenting with every shove.

A whimper escaped her lips, half moaned, half guttural sob. But her hips lurched to meet him all the same.

Betrayed by her body. By the gooey slick gushing from her sodden channel, squelching from her depths with every invasion of the colossus reshaping her insides.

Something was wrong.

Different.

There was no careful foreplay. No practiced, restrained ritual she could feel in his every movement. No burning ache of venom pulsing through her blood. His movements were utterly absent any hint of breathy hunger drawn out between clashing bodies.

There was only fury.

Claw digging into her hips, his thrusts nudged her forward, then dragged her back. Scraping her skin across the stone. "Pl-please! I-I can't—"

He snarled above her, misting her shoulders with spittle. And his claws—digging into muscle, too tight—dimpled her flesh with bruising force. Anchoring her in place, nailing her down as she was made to take the vengeful drive of a monster unmaking her in the dark.

Stone grinding against her cheek with every punishing stroke, Kore felt it building and knew she was doomed. Climax. Unholy lust for what he was doing to her. Inside her.

She reached and felt the shift between man and leviathan, fingers slipping against warm skin, then sharp scale. And, digits curling, she took what he rained down upon her. The sound of slapping flesh filled the cave. Obscene and wet.

It was always wet now.

She tried to twist, to peer at his face and understand.

"Why?" she whispered, desperate to know why it felt cruel this time. Like he was just a man enacting vengeance upon a woman's flesh, and not... not what he'd been *before*.

He didn't answer, of course.

Merely tore a sharp, broken sob from her throat.

Pussy fluttering, she clenched around him. Her belly stretched taut as she was sent hurtling toward the edge of that cliff, rounding with each brutal pump. The curve of it was obscene. Lewd. *Alive.*

Because his cock was too thick. Too long. Too gods damned much.

But she took it anyway.

Every last inch was gobbled up and milked for the pleasure only he could give.

Beast or not.

Cruel or kind.

Venom or lust.

It didn't matter.

The walls of her sodden cunt spasmed and sucked him deeper. A breathless chant rattling through slack jaws, she murmured, "Yes, yes, yes. Gods, give me more. Please, please, I'm almost—"

Snarling above her, breath ragged and bloody, he worked her over with single-minded intent.

Still, he drove her into the stone. Pulsing and shaking, as if desperate to fuck her full of sperm. To replace what she'd given to the sea.

Kore gasped as the bubble of ecstasy building between her hips bulged tighter, then burst. Her thighs flexed hard enough to shake as the world grew blurry at the edges. Climax washing over her, a grateful, ragged moan spilled from her lips.

She was full.

A wet grunt broke the silence.

Kore blinked, twisting, slow and stiff. Her spine arched in protest as she tried again to look.

And then she saw him.

Poseidon's son loomed above her. A god at the altar, a specter of war. Blood dripping in slow, syrupy pulses from the slashed vents of his gills. His every breath was heavy, a ragged rasp that sprayed her cheeks red as he gazed with glassy, sightless eyes.

He wasn't looking at her.

Not really.

No, his pupils were blown wide—his gaze slicing through her as he stared somewhere she couldn't see and wasn't invited to go.

It was a look she recognized.

His arms trembled where they bracketed her body, shoulders locked and straining as he fought the clenching waves of her climax, and began to thrust anew. Instinct driving him to empty his balls into her womb.

A gust of wind blew touseled, sweat-slicked hair around his face—and something massive and glittering slapped across her brow.

A scale.

Green and blue, speckled with purple iridescent flakes. This one as large as her palm.

She looked beyond clenched muscle, quivering belly, and saw… carnage.

The scales lining his tail were flaking off in glittering ribbons.

Blinking, dazed with the shock of an incredible climax, her brain was slow to grasp this new reality.

That his body, sculpted by gods, terrible yet divine… it was coming apart.

No matter that he'd fucked her like he was trying to outpace death.

The truth struck her with enough force to make her gasp.

He was dying.

It was there in the way his jaws gaped open, in the hair clinging to his forehead in dark strands. In the blood glistening where his gills fluttered and clapped, each gasping breath sending a red mist peppering the air between them. And his eyes—pupils yawning wide and inky black—they gleamed with an inhuman, feral intent.

Merciless and unyielding, obviously in excruciating pain.

Because he was dying.

And yet, he continued to breed her.

"What—what's happening to you?" she asked, voice a hoarse rasp edged with panic.

The beast only snarled.

Grinding against the most tender parts of a body that should have broken days ago. Her womb clenched, suckling at his tip. Begging for his offering.

"Please," she whispered, reaching to cup his cheek, her voice breaking. "Please stop."

Her body betrayed even that, hips rolling to meet his next thrust. Fluttering with the ache to be stretched. Owned. Ruined and remade.

It was his turn to groan, and it was a sound that made her eyes sting.

He was collapsing. Weight pressing her thighs wider still, his rhythm shuddering. Breath growing wetter as he choked on blood, and still—*still*—he drove himself in to the root. Forcing one final surge deep into her core.

It was the last.

With a snarl that lacked any whisper of finesse, he came.

An unholy sound that ripped through his chest and splattered against her shoulder. Wetting her cheek.

Sending a molten flood of cum rushing through the mouth of her womb.

Squealing, Kore tried to buck the pleasure stabbing through her with a broken, "Gods, I can't… Please… stop…"

A lie.

A floundering attempt at selflessness. The sort of chastity she was sworn to uphold.

It didn't stop her from climaxing as her womb ballooned with the volume. Body jerking with the waves of pleasure, her belly distended with the obscene fullness. Spine bowing, her cunt spasmed around him. Gaping. Clenching and milking. Training to take all he might give, and keep it sealed inside.

She saw the pain ripple across his face, marring his brow. Watching as his muscles clenched, his jaw bunching at the corner as he shivered above her.

Kore saw the effort it took, for she'd been raised to sacrifice. Trained to endure so others might prosper.

And she knew.

There was a price.

One paid so he could force her belly to grow fat and round, nearly brushing the stone floor as his thrusts grew slower.

Shallow, now.

As if each jab left a piece of himself behind.

And it did.

Her belly was stretched with the sheer impossible quantity of semen that pulsed and grew with every agonizing push.

Too much.

Too hot.

She collapsed beneath him, twitching on the stone. The curve of her gut swollen and absurd.

The beast lurched back, his cock slurping free with a grotesque, sucking *schlorp* that echoed off the cave walls.

Almost immediately, she felt his cum go from liquid to gel.

Reacting to the air, it left her plugged with seed. Stuffed and gaping around a seal of thick, clotted cream.

Fluttering where she was abandoned, soiled and shamed, spasming from the stretch, she could only blink when he wrenched himself away.

With a choked gasp, he narrowly avoided crushing her beneath his colossal weight as he flung his body toward the exit. Clawing his way to the surf.

Leaving a trail of glittering scales, spatters of brackish gore, and cooling seed, he lurched toward safety. A mighty, three-pronged weapon crashing into the stone as he moved.

Heavy, awkward undulations of his massive tail flicked across stone and sand as he struggled to return to his natural element. The thump of the trident echoed his desperation in every shuddering jolt.

He didn't make it.

The trident slipped from his grasp, landing with force enough to jiggle her fat as she watched, horrified when the beast went next.

Slumping as he fell.

Half in, half out of the water, he splashed into the surf.

A leviathan stranded on the beach.

Utterly motionless where he lay.

"Gods…" she whispered, pulsing with the aftershocks still rolling through her body. The scent of cum and blood still filled the damp air. Trembling in a puddle of cooling, congealing fluids, her entire body throbbed with the sordid work they'd done together.

And her brain, sluggish with numbed disbelief, was slow to acknowledge the horrific truth.

He was the *only* one, man or not, who knew where she was.

"Hey!" she called, voice trembling and breathy.

No response.

Just a fragile shudder of his fins, trembling in the ocean breeze. Water lapped at his edges, but that was all.

Her breath caught. Snagged on something dreadful at the back of her throat. Something ancient and cold that bloomed in her heart and thrashed at the back of her ribs.

"No," she rasped, staggering to her knees. Bones turned to jelly, dripping with the evidence of what he'd done to her—of what they'd done... *together*—she pulsed with the glow. Skin rosy and flushed.

But her eyes were locked to him. Rimmed in white.

Forcing herself to her feet, balance tipped too far aft, she swayed on untrustworthy legs. Then, grinding her molars, she forced a sliver of steel through her blood, clambered over slick rock, and moved.

It was a slog to stumble down the beach. No matter that she'd grown accustomed to the fundamental change in her balance after each session with the beast, she staggered and tripped. Fighting the pain.

"Don't... don't you *dare* die now," she said, injecting venom into her throat as she dragged herself down the slope of stone and sand. "You don't get to f-fuck me like that, and then die, you wretched bastard. Not after"—she gasped for breath, one hand on her swollen girth, the other flailing for balance—"not after all *that.*"

When she reached him, she went to her knees in the surf. Splashing down beside him, absent any hint of grace.

Nothing.

Not a flinch or a twitch.

No reaction that might offer a glimmer of hope.

Panic flared in her chest. Throttling her breath where it was trapped at the back of her throat. If he died here... if she was left marooned on this lonely spit of rock and sand... How would she eat? How would she *leave*? As monstrous as he was... he'd fed her.

Watched her. *Needed* her enough that he'd risk everything just for another chance to pump her full.

Crawling, Kore shuffled closer. Helplessly fascinated by his alien shape.

Breath hitching, she paused to look—truly look.

He was huge.

Even unconscious, pure, raw power radiated off his skin. Shimmering and blinding beneath the cruel glare of the sun.

Scales.

Entranced, she reached and did not look at the same glitter sparkling beneath her own skin.

Because his scales weren't just flaking away… they were shedding. Sliding off his skin in sheets, to reveal a soft membrane beneath. Fragile. Raw… bleeding.

His gills flapped, wet and rattling. A breath lifted his chest, and it was shallow. Agonized.

Fingers brushing his shoulder, Kore touched the divine. Tracing the line of muscle coiled between elbow and wrist, before she prodded the webbing between clawed digits.

At the contact, his fins flared. Splayed wide and trembling, but that was all. A passive threat from the most dangerous creature she'd ever known.

"I don't… don't know what to do," she admitted. "I should leave. Escape now, before…"

She swallowed.

Took a breath.

And then… "Don't"—her voice cracked—"Don't leave me," she whispered and touched his gills with a single, outstretched finger.

It twitched.

Reflexive.

Still alive.

"Please," she said, choking on a broken sob. "I—I don't know how to do this without you. Can't. *Can't* do this without you," she admitted, because it was true.

Not the breeding.

No, men had shown her just how cheap and insignificant a commodity the female body really was.

It was... everything else.

Water frothed around them, splashing pink and foamy where it washed away another row of scales.

Helpless to resist, fascinated by the morbid, she touched where he'd been left stripped.

Warm.

Shockingly so. His skin soft. Delicate. Thinner than she'd thought possible. Vulnerable where the armoured plating of scales was absent.

But his body was falling apart.

He'd pushed too hard.

Given too much in the quest to mark her. Spent too much time above the surface when he was meant for the sea.

Pressing her forehead to his chest, Kore took a breath of the brine clinging to his skin. Listening to his heart thump.

She had to try.

Even if it was hopeless.

Desperate.

Jaw bunching, Kore slipped her fingers beneath his forearm, set her feet in the wet sand, and lifted.

She couldn't so much as budge his arm.

Dragging him into the sea would be utterly impossible.

Sweating freely, Kore swallowed the lump of panic and looked for something—anything—she might use.

The trident.

Already half-sunk into the sand, thrumming with an ominous energy, but almost three times her height.

With a huff, she collapsed in the sand beside him, her belly swollen and heavy. Her chest heaving with the effort, breaths growing ragged with panic.

It was almost funny, the games gods played. The things they demanded mortals to do in the name of service.

Entranced, almost helpless to resist, Kore allowed herself to succumb to the curiosity. To touch what had been her doom, inspect the monster who'd claimed her. She was drawn to the hypnotic glimmer of a blue-green glow humming beneath the surface where his scales had sloughed away.

So different.

So alien.

She touched a fin, gasping when it flared. Almost stabbing her with a spine before it lay flat once more.

"Beautiful," she murmured, voice a low hum of interest. And, letting her fingers down his forearm, she marveled at the delicate patterns etched in his skin. The delicate webbing between clawed digits, lax in his crisis. Deadly and sharp.

He didn't move.

Didn't snap or snarl or seethe.

Growing bold, Kore's touch drifted to the taut ridge of abdominal muscles. Searching for a flinch, a twitch, anything that might indicate his divinity. That he could survive.

For both of them.

This was wrong.

Immoral.

Taboo and obscene.

She should flee.

But her hand was already moving, already sliding toward the seam below his navel, where man and leviathan became one.

Curiosity was a devious mistress.

Her fingers hovered before sliding… lower.

To the line of scales that guarded his cock. The seam was subtle. Ridged and muscular.

She ran her fingers along its edge, tracing the line with a quiet reverence.

It pulsed.

Her mouth watered.

And his cock twitched. Sluggish, at first. Slow. His slit opening to reveal the tip, glistening in the light. Thick and wet with a moisture all its own.

"Maybe this will be enough," Kore rasped, her throat parched and dry. Eyes fixed to the serpent too exhausted to fully emerge from its den, she grew bold. Pressing at his seam, she followed the trunk of his cock in.

It was warm inside.

Moist.

Slick.

Sucking a breath between her teeth, she pressed deeper. Circling her fingers around his base, her grip tightened as she followed him back. Sinking inside. Entranced as her knuckles disappeared.

Then her wrist.

The glimmer of blue-green scales a stunning contrast for those that gleamed with the glory of a sunrise.

He was heavy inside. Huge. And growing larger as she worked.

Pumping, twisting, she dragged her palm back, then drove deeper.

There should have been shame. Disgust. Fear. Something, *anything*, but the slippery heat building low in her belly. But her thumb stroked the glans, slow and measured, and his body answered.

A shiver rolled down his spine. Fins flaring to reveal the point of deadly, toxic spines leaking the venom she'd come to know so well. And cum. It beaded at his tip as the monster flexed and bulged in her fist.

She blinked.

Licking dry lips.

And when she bent low, breath fanning over the head of him, it was to inhale the musk of salt and venom.

She couldn't help but taste him.

After all…

… it had been days since she'd last eaten.

And gods help her… she was starving…

CHAPTER 19

The pain struck him first.

Everywhere all at once. Searing hot, it was a living thing both desperate and ravenous. It feasted on flaking scales, charred skin, and eyes singed by the cruel glare of the sun. Every contour and curve. Every delicate filament and gossamer fin.

His was to be a brutal death.

And then his awareness sharpened.

Warm. Wet. *Hot.*

She was there.

His human bride.

On her knees, tangled hair falling around his hips in lank clumps as she licked and kissed and sucked.

Sucking.

She moaned, his little slut. Making a vacuum where her lips were sealed around the ridged flare of his cock, she drew up a throbbing, molten pulse of cum.

And then her fingers moved.

Not the ones wrapped around his girth—through those were busy pumping another dollop of cream onto her greedy little tongue.

No, she was *inside his vent*. It was invasive, so desperately, incredibly wrong to feel a tiny human hand buried to the wrist inside his slit. Pumping his cock at the base, where his girth was still hidden in that protective pocket. She kneaded what had not yet fully emerged, where his knot ached to balloon inside her tiny human pussy and lock her in place as he bred her full of his spawn.

Ravaged gills flared, dragging pure, blistering air into his soggy lungs.

"Mmmm," she hummed, fingers pumping him inside and out. "Thank the gods. You're awake. *Alive.*" Pupils luminous despite the harsh glare of the sun gleamed up at him as she dropped her mouth back to his prick. Wet heat enveloped him. Sucking, blinding heat.

Her tongue curled beneath the flare of his helm, tracing the ridged seam of flesh—almost enough to draw his pearls out. To make them bulge and throb where they lay dormant in the ridges of his shaft.

Throat clicking, he swallowed. Vision tunneling as he stared at Kore and watched her work. Nursing on his cock.

Instinct seized him, then.

Despite the agony, his body locked, every nerve snapping taut. Fins flaring, his spines flicked up. A defensive posture outside of his control, one meant to stabilize him in the current, to posture and warn that *he* was the most deadly thing in the sea. Venomous. Powerful.

Deadly.

Slippery fingers found the heavy globes of his balls, where they were hidden inside. Concealed and protected by muscle and scale.

Nyx uttered a defensive snarl, even as another molten gush of seed gurgled up to fill her mouth. Gills flaring in the dry air issued a low, helpless groan beneath the rush of sensation.

Sending blood rushing through his skull, pounding against the delicate membranes meant for the deep.

He couldn't breathe. Couldn't blink.

He could only watch as human lips slid lower, forcing him past that tight ring of muscle at the back of her slender throat with a series of obscene *clicks*.

And then she swallowed.

Pressure built in his slit, and guided by dainty human hands working inside his vent, his sack burst into the cruel sunlight. Coaxed by human touch. Heavy, despite being so recently emptied, his balls had grown swollen and ripe. Skin pulled taut. Shiny with the volume sloshing inside.

And then she pulled back, letting his cock slither free. Bumping over every ridge of her throat, every ring of cartilage felt at the base of his spine.

A string of pre-cum mixed with the dew of her saliva—he blinked.

Beautiful.

The most hypnotic sight he'd ever seen.

More. He needed more.

Without being told, she obliged. Lips stretching, she worked her mouth down. Teeth scraping, tongue worming, she inched him toward the back of her throat, and back. Miming what he needed to climax, slippery drool spilled and globbed at the tight seal of lips on cock.

Sharp, glorious sensation burst behind his eyes. Pain and pleasure blended in a furious swirl that saw the trident react, humming with the thirst for war where it had been forgotten in the sand.

But Nyx couldn't look away.

Cock throbbing, his tail twitched, spines fanning against sand. Testing the limits of his scorched and blistered hide. Need—a deep, visceral thing—pulsed in his veins. The primal urge to drag her into the surf, shove inside that tiny human slit, and knot her placid as he made her bulge with enough seed to keep her breeding for him.

But he was too weak.

Too damaged for the sport of breeding her for entertainment, this was survival. Cold, calculated, selfish.

Hips jerking, the flat of his tail fin slapped the sand. It was a motion that sent another bolt of pain rippling through him, but drove his prick toward the back of her throat. Begging to be sheathed in that tight glove of pleasure.

A moan spattered over his length as he flexed and pumped a gush of brine over her palate. Pulling back just enough to coat her tongue in a thick glob of sperm.

"Gods," she whispered, her breath misting over his throbbing tip. Voice ragged and low, her pupils massive disks of flat black. She glanced up at him, tiny fingers traveling over his length. Hands too small to circle his girth, but still, she worked him. "That's it," she murmured, shuffling closer on her knees. Belly too swollen for anything approaching grace. "More. Give it to me, beast."

It tore a rumble from his chest. Weak. A subsonic purr she couldn't hear, for it was beyond her frail human senses. Still, another slick pulse of cum leaked out to feed his bride.

She suckled at his tip, tongue darting out to lap up the slime before Kore took him deeper once more. Groaning. Sending a vibration of her own down his shaft.

Stars burst behind his eyes. Tail flexing, spines flaring a warning that went unheeded when she fucked her own throat, bobbing and slurping over his cock.

Hissing, Nyx tensed with the surge boiling inside.

A roar exploded from his throat. Unexpected, savage, his hand shot forward. Clawed fingers tangled in her hair, anchoring at the base of her skull.

He shoved.

Burying his cock down her throat in one vicious thrust, he sheathed himself in all that was welcoming and wet. Warm.

A tiny sound escaped her then, muffled. Surprised discomfort when he anchored her in place and let his cock explore her throat.

But she didn't struggle.

Remade to take, her body tensed for an instant. She gagged, eyes watering as she looked at him, blinked, then yielded. Swallowing to milk his shaft.

That was all it took.

His hips snapped, back arching as he came. Cum erupted from him in thick, viscous waves. Each pulse gurgling from heavy balls that flexed with the effort to fill her belly. Cock buried deep enough that she couldn't taste her meal, he spent himself down her throat.

And then, claws gentling as he emptied his balls, he groomed the tangles of matted hair. Rewarding Kore for taking every gulp.

When it was done, he didn't release her. Wasn't quite ready to give up the soft seal of her lips, nor the silken grip of the windpipe that took him so well.

He dragged her back with deliberate control. Letting her lips snag over his bulging pearls as he pulled free.

A soft gasp spilled from her wrecked throat, lips puffy with vigor. Spit and sperm dribbled from a slack jaw, wetting her chin and chest.

And, eyes wide—luminous—she stared back at him with something approaching awe.

Mine.

The trident hummed, thrumming with ominous heat. Starving for the battle. Ready to stake a claim that could not be unwritten until the seas ran dry.

Nyx frowned, tearing his eyes from Kore's to glance at the ancient weapon.

It was an artifact of war.

A symbol of conquest.

That it reacted to her was… fitting.

Prophetic.

Wrapping one hand around her throat, Nyx shook her. Gentle. Firm. His fingers ringed her skinny neck, claws clicking at her nape. Forging a collar of unspoken threat. It was a command written in flesh dimpled by claws, just enough to make her *listen* to what went unsaid.

He dragged her closer, up past his retreating cock. Over the flat plane of his belly, until she was draped snug over his chest. Blinking down at him with wide, shocked eyes.

And then, with his free hand, he cupped her belly.

Where she was swollen. Full. Heavy and bloated with his seed. Filled from both ends.

He let his claws score that shiny skin, flexing with a possessive snarl and an unblinking glare.

A warning.

Keep it.

Claws flexing, spreading wide across the curve of a belly that would soon be ripe with life, he let a rumble jiggle her marrow with pure, unfiltered menace.

Uttering a tiny kiss of the Resonance, he purred for her. Just a little. For half a breath before it stuttered and stopped.

But she heard him anyway.

Understood just how deeply he wanted to drag her into the surf. Breed her until water filled her lungs. Until she was his, forever.

The effort to indulge his temper—to go to battle with the *Thalassari* king? It had depleted the last of his reserves. Nyx released her, allowing her to pull away.

For a long moment, there was only the rasp of harsh breaths and the rush of the sea calling him back.

And then, "Go," she whispered, not daring to move. The single syllable hitching in her ravaged throat. Cunt glistening, swollen and wet, left needy and ripe. But still, she dared to command him. "Go back," she said again. "Before you die and leave me here to rot."

He was burning.

Flayed by the sun. Poisoned by the surface. Every inch of him blistered. Gills savaged and dripping, scales flaking from his body in glinting, iridescent ribbons—armor peeling from meat.

He should have waited.

Recovered.

He'd ascended in a rage to punish his bride—and instead... she'd stitched him back together.

Rumbling, he seized the trident and turned to obey. Tail dragging behind him, bunching and shifting as he struggled back to the surf and carved a trench in the sand. The trident was too heavy to lift, too sacred to abandon. His chest heaved with effort, gills flapping open in desperate need as he worked deeper.

Every inch gained was easier. Weightless. Welcoming. The tide embraced him. Lapping at his wounds with the promise of salvation.

Nyx turned, just once, at the edge of the sea.

She was watching.

Hair tangled and wild. Lips red, swollen, glistening with him. Her belly—heavy and round—was marked where he'd touched her so much deeper than she could possibly know.

His command echoed in the wind between them.

Don't spill a drop.

Nyxarion let the trident fall, the weight of it dragging him down when he collapsed forward into the surf and vanished beneath the waves in a flick of seafoam and shadow.

The sea enveloped him. A desperate embrace that sank into every blister. Sloughing flaking scales away as he descended, and left a trail of glittering gore twirling through the current.

Ribs aching with the twist of his spine, gills fluttering with the blissful burn of salt.

Yawning wide beneath him, the trench emerged from the dark.

He let it swallow him. Let it hurt.

The trident dragged him down, allowing him to conserve his energy as he sank through the anoxic layers, through the burning acid where nothing could thrive.

And when he was close enough to see the hint of his reef glowing below, he let the trident slip from his fingers. Watched it crash into the seabed, thinking not of rutting or claiming his bride, nor the slow extinction of the *Abyssari* who had exiled him.

Fins flaring to slow his descent, Nyx's body was a ruin. Too weak to answer when the coral polyps reached out in silent greeting that went unanswered.

No, for the first time in eons, he wasn't thinking of war. Or vengeance. He thought only of a soft slip of a girl. A human who'd taken him into her throat and begged him to go, if only so he might return.

Kore.

His living flame.

His vessel.

A girl who knelt in the spume with his cock in her mouth and hands on her swollen belly, promising not to spill a drop.

He grinned.

Aroused beyond his wildest fantasies. Enthralled, because she might just live long enough to rule the Black Sea at his side…

CHAPTER 20

Blinking awake, Kore shifted back to consciousness. Groggy and gasping, spine rattling against stone.

Silence.

Not peace. Not safety.

Just the absence of deep, rattling breath. Of scales slapping skin.

Alone.

He was gone.

It should have brought relief. Instead? Dread hummed in the back of her mind. The memory of that ravaged body, limp and all but lifeless in the surf, sinking into the deep.

Heat kissed her cheeks when she thought of what she'd done to bring him back. That she'd slipped her hand inside him to draw that colossus... out. Feasting on the taste of him, she'd gulped him down. Her hands were slick when she'd rolled massive, heavy balls through the tight slit guarding his genitals. Coaxing them into the air.

To save him.

She'd done it... to save him.

Clenching, her pussy remembered the lie.

And her body... *Gods.*

Her thighs were sticky. Bruised. Pussy swollen and tender, aching from the inside out. Her throat was dry. Sore. Fucked raw.

Brine lingered on her palate. Salt burning in every crevice, sand stuck in places the sun priests of Delphi had never thought to warn her about.

Stretching, Kore reached toward the sea—and froze.

There was something stuck between her fingers.

Rolling around her belly, Kore sat up. Slow. Stiff. Her every movement a reminder of the monster who'd marked her, but one she ignored as she stared at her hands.

Webbing.

Delicate, gossamer petals stretched between her spread fingers.

Just a pearlescent shimmer, but the skin was tender. Reddened. Sensitive and painful, the skin between each digit was swollen with a blister ready to split.

Horror made her stomach churn, but she prodded the delicate membrane with one trembling finger.

Sensation lit her nerves with an electric reality.

She was growing webbing between her fingers.

Standing, Kore wobbled into the blinding glare of the sun. Hissing against the bright light, she stretched her fingers, wide as they might go—and saw the glitter of scales breaking through the skin.

"Please," she whispered through a broken sob. "Gods, *no.*"

Her voice was wrong. Hoarse and ravaged. But that was to be expected, wasn't it? After what she'd done? After what she'd swallowed?

Licking cracked lips, Kore lifted someone else's hands to her brow. Hiding sensitive eyes from the sun. Heart beating through her chest, pounding behind her eyes, felt in the puffy, tender skin aching all over her body. Everything that throbbed and screamed for attention, all at once.

Her jaw flexed. Sore at the corners.

Not with bruises, not from gaping wide around a cock that had no business plumbing her throat.

It was something else. An internal twinge that flexed with her every breath.

She'd done damage to herself, then. Broken something essential when she'd let him fuck himself empty down her throat.

There'd been a purpose in her madness. A need beyond filling her belly, or dying alone on this forgotten spit of land.

Kore crouched, hands braced and spread wide in the sand. Trying not to see the alien glitter of scales, nor the webbing stretched taut between her fingers, she hiccuped. Belly tight, too full, distended.

She retched. Stringy bile splashed into the sand, but that was all.

Because she'd already absorbed what he'd pumped into her gut. Already made him a part of her. It was right there, in the sparkle growing beneath her skin, in the ocean of sperm sealed away inside her treacherous cunt.

He was inside her, this beast from the deep.

Changing her from the inside out.

Wiping her hand against her thigh, she braced herself for this new reality.

That he might not come back.

Might already be dead, drifting somewhere in the current.

And if he was?

She would soon follow. Marooned alone on a spit of rock in the middle of a forgotten, nameless sea.

Gritting her teeth, Kore turned and staggered into the cool embrace of the dark—and tripped over a pile of stones.

The tide markers.

Rocks she'd piled at the edge of the tide to time his absence between... *sessions.*

A breathless laugh escaped her, then, and she pressed her hand flat to the wall of the cave.

The tide was at its lowest point. Water lapping at stones well below the edge of the sandy beach.

The beast was ravaged by his own nefarious purposes, his fate unknown.

And the cave... it was a sanctuary from the sun for as long as it took for her to starve, or... worse.

Then? The cave would become her coffin.

"No," Kore said again, but this time, there was fire in the denial. "Not for me."

He'd left her with a belly bulging with promise, the command to keep what he'd sewn obvious, even without a shared language between them.

Dragging herself over to the deepest tidal pool, way in the back of the cave, Kore paused at the edge. Eyes fixed to the gentle ripple of the water trapped in a shallow basin, and not... not the reflection of a girl she didn't know staring back at her.

It would hide her lie.

Give her the time she needed to escape, so the beast couldn't smell himself in the current and return with punishment in his heart.

She slipped into the cool water.

Spread her legs.

Sending trembling fingers down, over the foreign swell of her belly, she touched what he'd left slimy and slick with shame. Spread puffy petals with two fingers, then dipped inside.

Cold and sharp, salt water rushed inside, and her body bucked against the shock of intrusion.

A guttural moan tore free of her lips, making the damage in her throat flutter and kick at the corner of her jaw. A low, shocked sound she didn't recognize as human.

The salt stung. Lighting nerves she didn't know she had, with a pleasure she wasn't sure existed.

She found it quickly. The plug. Wedged inside her, a grotesque mockery of the maidenhead she'd given to a god who'd never bothered to answer her prayers.

Grunting, Kore sent her fingers deeper, spreading those digits wide to let the sea creep inside.

"Take it back," she groaned, curling her fingers. "Please. Take it... back..."

Pumping, she guided the salty water toward the plug, pressing against that spongy head glued inside her.

And felt it melt.

Dissolving in slow, sickening gushes, ropes of sperm spilled into the tidal pool, floating on the surface with an oily sheen. Thick and cloudy, milk-white smoke curling through the water.

She watched it.

Couldn't look away. Utterly hypnotized by the sheer volume that came pouring from between her thighs.

Fingers working of their own accord, rough with the scrape of new scales, she explored her pussy.

She came.

Unexpected. Violent.

An orgasm shattered what little remained of her modesty—her body was seized in a fist of blinding pleasure. Hips bucking, the fingers of her free hand curled around the edge of the pool as she spasmed and lurched. Bearing down as each wave of climax crashed through her nerves, Kore sent another torrent of sperm splashing into the water.

Until the tidal pool churned with it.

Until she was empty.

Purged.

Sweating, she took a breath that ached below her ears and stood on legs that had gone jiggly and loose. Belly flat, pressure gone, she staggered toward the mouth of the cave with steel in her blood.

The sun was merciless above.

Unforgiving, blister-bright heat lashed her shoulders, peeling at her skin in angry ribbons.

Kore walked anyway.

Clambering over rocks exposed by low tide and slick with algae, she moved with a purpose. Away from the last place she'd seen that monstrous tail fluke slip beneath the waves. Stumbling over barnacles until her feet were raw, she marched through seaweed that clung.

And then, trembling and sick, she stepped into the sea.

Splashing into frigid water with a hiss, Kore didn't look back.

Not once.

Offering no last glance at the cave where she'd been imprisoned, she simply walked until she reached the edge of her tiny world.

Until a shelf of coastal bedrock dropped away, where the beach bled into the abyss, and there was nothing but the sea and sky. Seafoam hissing at her back, the yawning blackness of the bottomless deep below her.

It was hypnotic, the abyss. A lure that beckoned her to slip under and know what it was to be *him*.

Salt washed over her lips, flooding her throat and burning chapped lips. Kore plunged beneath the waves, the chill striking her with a slap as ice washed over blistered flesh.

She choked on a gasp. Her throat caught on at the edges of the shock.

Body seizing, muscles locked, lurched toward the surface. Bursting through into the air, she sobbed as she choked. Terrified screams cawing over a ravaged voice, left breathless in the chill, she dipped beneath the surface again.

Only once. Just long enough to see the fathomless black and feel the weight of the deep for what it really was.

Endless.

Her limbs thrashed in an ugly, graceless panic. Legs thrashing. Muscles screaming as agony speared through her bones.

But she didn't stop.

She kicked again, *hard.*

Spreading her fingers, an instinct seized her as she clawed toward the surface. The water grew thick in her hands, caught in a grip no longer quite human, she was propelled to the surface with a speed that made her gasp.

The water gave.

Parting around her as she sliced through, gliding as she burst through to the surface. Sucking in a breath that ached and burned at the back of her jaw, Kore blinked the salt from her eyes and kept swimming.

And swimming.

Eyes glassy and fixed to the distant horizon. Where waves crashed against the swollen underbelly of blackened storm clouds.

Swimming, swimming, *swimming.*

Absent purpose or direction.

One stroke after the next.

She lost track of time. Her body and mind. Everything drifted with the current, caught in the lull of waves and the burn in her shoulders.

There was nothing but the next kick. The next stroke.

She swam through pain and fear.

Not strong or fast. Absent grace or wild, determined purpose.

She simply moved with whatever remained in a dying body until her arms dragged through the water in weakened arcs. Until her jaws sagged on ragged gasps, as the sea flooded her throat and burned her lungs.

One kick.

Another.

Her body moving for nothing but a shred of fragile instinct that commanded survival. Growing weaker with every lurch toward a destination that offered no hope.

No distant sighting of land.

The horizon mocked her. Taunting her with an endless wash of grey turning black. As the sun turned away from her plight, and the night swallowed anything that might've once felt like hope.

Fingers aching as she cut through the water, Kore felt the webbing stretch with every stroke.

And *gods...* she was so tired.

Her head dipped under.

For a heartbeat. Two.

The water held her in an embrace, cradled.

Spluttering, she surfaced with a gasp. Shoulders burning, muscles screaming for her to stop. To give in and just... find peace.

She coughed again and felt it ripple beneath the corner of her jaw, but the sound was hollow. Empty. The particular tang of iron flooded her mouth, metallic and sharp.

A wave slapped her.

Something brushed her thigh. Soft. Silken.

A fragile, weak scream tore through her reedy throat. The sound was barely a whisper.

Legs jerking, she tried to kick and thrash, but her limbs had grown leaden. Too heavy. Weighted down by the promise pulling her into the gloom.

Her head dipped again.

She let it.

Blinking, she found the salt didn't burn her eyes so badly anymore. And she watched the last light of the sun as it shimmered above. Distorted by the waves.

Below her, in the deep blue abyss, something cold twisted around her knee. Slipping lower, to caress her ankles before it was swept away—a lure, the promise of what lay below her.

Dragged down, floating just beneath the surface, she tried to kick but couldn't rise. Buoyant. Cocooned by the sea.

Wrapped in seafoam and shadow.

Just as her sisters had been. Drowned at the bottom of the Aegean, dragged to the bottom by an Athenian trireme.

It came slow, the realization. The sense of the familiar was a sluggish memory that teased at the edge of her mind, for she'd been here before.

And it hadn't been an escape.

It was a new beginning.

She let her body sink.

A wave crested, sending her tumbling, forcing her up for just a moment. Enough for her to take a shocked breath of air before she was pushed under once more.

The sea seeped between her lips, slicked her throat, spilling into her lungs in tiny sips that made her insides burn.

Below... blackness that was somehow... welcoming, despite the profound absence. No bedrock or limit. Just an infinite, yawning scream. An ancient hunger that throbbed with a living heartbeat she could feel thrumming through her marrow.

Beckoning.

Closing her eyes against the void, Kore let her head fall back as the warmth was washed away from her fingers and toes.

This was how her sisters had died.

Left to the tide, swallowed whole. Sacrificed for a deity who'd turned away from their desperate prayers.

Thunk.

The sound echoed, forcing her eyes to snap open.

Thunk.

It was the dull slap of wood on wood.

Thunk.

Foreign and jarring. A sound that had no business in the middle of this forgotten sea where she was meant to drown. Forgotten. Cold.

Thunk.

CHAPTER 21

She was drowning.

The tide lapped soft against her skin, a glove of velvet deception that was almost... gentle. Close enough to sweet to be a believable lie.

Thunk.

Her throat opened around a scream—and the sea rushed in.

A shadow passed overhead. And then the splatter of something heavy splashed above her.

Rope.

A net.

The weight descended, folding around her like a shroud.

She was dragged up through the waves. Heavy and pulling against the current that clung to her every sodden inch and tried to keep her under.

And when she breached the surface, it was to the sound of a male voice grunting with the effort to haul her up from the abyss.

"Gods, half-drowned already," the man grunted, bringing her alongside the tiny boat. The vessel rocked as he worked, wood groaning and creaking. "Heavy little relic, ain't ya?" he asked,

172

then pulled her up. Cursing and huffing as the boat rocked under her weight.

She hit the deck with a splat of waterlogged limbs. Trying to breathe, hardly able to lift her head as she blinked at the man who'd rescued her after hours of aimless swimming.

Coarse hands landed on her, then. Callused, roughened in the way of seafarers. Those hardened men who handled rope and seashells for an honest living.

He grabbed at her without reverence, pawing at slick skin and tattered robes that clung to her body and did absolutely nothing to shield her modesty.

"Ain't the first thing I've pulled from these waters," he murmured, thumbing the swell of her hip. Brushing the glitter of sunrise scales fanning out above her pubis. "But fuck me raw if you ain't the prettiest."

Kore blinked, but that was all. Unable to focus on his words. The dusk was too bright, the scent of fish—of rot and stale brine —curdled in her gut and promised to splash against the back of her throat.

"Roll for me, pretty thing," he said, gruff as he shoved at her hip. Fingers taking liberties, he tugged aside the scraps of her robes and left her bound in the netting at the bottom of his dinghy. "Gods," he rasped. "A real fine beaut."

Breath rattling and wet, lungs soggy, Kore tried to protest. Tried to resist when blunt, rough fingers explored her body.

Her lips parted, but issued no sound.

Throat reedy and dry, breath a phantom whisper.

Beneath her, the net crunched. Salt crackling and coarse. Dried into the fibers.

His hand slid lower, tracing the shimmer on her ribs. The faint gleam dusted across her chest, the point of her nipples. Her thighs... her... sex.

Everywhere she'd been marked by a beast was explored with quiet reverence.

And then his hand slid lower still, two fingers parting the lips of her slit. Marveling at how bare she was. Hairless. How slick and smooth. "Already leaking," he laughed, an incredulous lilt to his gruff voice. "Waiting on me, were ya?"

Curling around herself, Kore tried to twist. Gagging when her lungs seized and her breath strangled high at the back of her throat, aching beneath the corner of her jaws.

"Wai—" she hissed, voice a wisp of smoke and broken glass, throat too raw to muster a fragile protest, much less an outraged scream.

"Aye, treasure," he said, hands prodding. "I'll get ya sorted, beastie. Bet on that."

An ache started low, a shuddering throb that wasn't quite pain.

It was *need*.

Starvation.

Confusion flooded her brain when her womb clenched. Her pussy flushing wet and open, desperate for something she didn't have, but needed more than the blistering air that ached when it sliced through her throat and burned in her lungs.

The fisherman laughed low, fingers working at her seam. "Oh, you're a desperate little cunny, alright. Caught a proper Siren, eh?"

Kore gasped as pain spiked through her blood.

And then she knew.

Understood the particular sort of ache turning her blood to fire.

She was bound.

Not by rope, but… biology. By what the beast had done to her on that island.

What he'd made her.

She clenched—slick, grasping, obscene. Body starving, keening for what she'd come to need. The soothing burn of that fevered ecstasy that had been pumped into her body, remaking her as something monstrous.

Venom.

She'd fled when the tide was low.

The last taste of his venom was days ago… a barb in her palm.

Not nearly enough.

Already her body was breaking. Cracking at the seams that hadn't been plugged in *hours.*

The fisherman didn't notice the desperate twitching—he pressed a palm to her belly. Marveling at the fever heating her glittering skin.

Lips gaping, she arched into his touch. Starved for the toxin she'd come to crave.

"Aye, lass. I know. You need it, don't you?" he asked, more curious than cruel. And then, "You'll sing for me. Soon, treasure," he crooned, slipping a finger back, twisting through her slick before he brought that digit to his lips and sucked. "By the drowned gods…" he groaned, fisting a bulge in his pants with his free hand. "Sweetest cunny I ever tasted."

Kore could only tremble. Arching, her hips canting into that touch without meaning to do it. Her thighs grew slick, flushed with a desperate want she didn't own. Didn't understand.

Pulling at his bloated little prick, he laughed, cheeks flushed. "Your tricks ain't gonna work, treasure. Not on me. I know your sort. Heard the tales all my life, understand? I know ye will try to drag me under with that sweet little trap between your legs. I know," he said, and didn't pull himself free of his pants. "Know what you're about. Luring good men into the sea by their cocks with a cursed cunny, begging to be fucked. Draggin' honest men into the dark, screamin'. Sent to their deaths for nothin' but the want of a taste of pussy they *earned.* Honest day's work."

Kore's lips parted when she tried to deny his fantasy. She wasn't a Siren! Just a woman in need of rescue.

But his fingers didn't stop.

And the ache grew, blooming into agony.

First two fingers, then three. Rubbing circles into her clit as her pussy gushed slick and her hips rocked against the friction.

She whimpered, a hoarse, cracked sound dragged from the bottom of soggy lungs, too ruined to scream. Teeth clenching, slicing, aching pain erupted behind the corner of her jaw.

"Wetter than the sea," he breathed, setting the sail to catch the wind. And then he shoved two fingers inside. Slick gushing around his digits, obscene and eager *and not meant for him.* "Oh, yeah," he crowed, watching her writhe with a sick, brown grin stretched wide over rotten teeth. "Made for this, ain't that right? Made to be bred, huh?"

She shook her head when her voice failed her. A twitch of denial too small to matter, for it didn't stop him. He only drove his fingers faster, working tight, graceless circles around the base of her clit. Delighting in her hips jerking and dancing at his command as he sailed toward a destination she could not see.

A sob tore free of her throat—silent and reedy—a gurgle of horror for the monstrous hunger consuming her in unholy flames.

Her body convulsed, forced toward the cliff of a climax she didn't want but couldn't resist.

Because it wouldn't help.

"Gonna ride you good," he groaned, still circling her clit. "Fuck you like a man. *On land.* Where you can't give me to some cursed sea demon."

Curling into the bottom of his boat, net digging into tender skin, Kore shuddered through a weak climax that only ignited the desperate need in her nerves.

"Almost there," he hummed, abandoning her slit to haul on the rudder.

They hit the shore with a thud.

Cursing, the fisherman jumped into the shallow water, huffing as he dragged the boat higher on the sandy beach.

Kore tried to thrash, tried to fight the netting as the last of the sun's heat retreated across the sea. As night curled around her with a velvet hiss, a distant glimmer of stars twinkled in the endless black high above.

Reaching into the boat, the fisherman snagged the netting and hauled her up. Out. Sweating, he pulled her over the edge of the gunwale with a careless thump of soggy, boneless limbs.

She hit the sand hard.

"Hush now, beastie," he hummed, stooping to bind her tighter in the netting, then dragged her across the shore. Taking delight in her ragged breaths, in the wide, glassy eyes with pupils blown wide.

Impact.

Her belly hit a log of driftwood with a splat.

Grunting, the fisherman bent her in half, adjusting her hips until she was, "Perfect. Aye," he murmured, agreeing with whatever it was he saw. "Exactly the treasure I thought ye to be."

Lips sagging, Kore hissed a wordless protest as the net cut into her wrists and elbows, chaffing her hips, her ribs. Digging into tender flesh as she was positioned across a log, hips raised for only one thing.

There was a moment of stillness.

The wind blew through her, chilling wet flesh, and she looked back. Turning wide, helpless eyes upon the man, she saw it.

Scales. A sea of stars glittering in the night, sprinkled across her thighs and wrists. Her lower back and upturned ass.

And there, beneath her skin…

… pulsing blue veins, throbbing in time with her frantic heart.

She was changed.

Alien.

A… a Siren.

Stepping back, admiring his handiwork, a smirk split the fisherman's weathered face. "Now that's a sight, ain't it?"

Kore didn't respond. Couldn't beg around a throat shredded by desperate want of the sea. She understood now.

Too late.

The man didn't care.

He wrapped a fist around his grubby little cock and stroked himself at the sight of her. Taking her in.

"Gonna give you exactly what you need, pretty thing," he said, stepping forward. "None o'that now," he murmured when she thrashed and showed her teeth. "Gonna take what I'm owed." His cock nudged her entrance. Prodding. Pressing against a slit that had betrayed her, time and again.

The head pushed in.

It was shameful, the way she gushed. Appalling just how desperate she was for the stretch, the primal command that had sent her to her knees in the sand, daring to feast at the beast's cock. Drinking down every last gulp of cream until her belly was swollen with it.

Oblivious, the fisherman stood behind her, mashing his rigid digit into her clenching slit. Small. Pathetic. Nowhere near enough.

He was grinning.

Rapturous.

Rutting at her upturned ass, spoiling the treasure he'd found with reckless abandon—because he didn't know. That the mess between her legs wasn't for him. That she'd been reshaped for another, and this trespass?

It was nothing.

A fingertip through a spiderweb.

An irritant she hadn't invited, one that served only to inflame her need for the leviathan lurking in the deep.

Kore sobbed, soundless. Keening as he slipped inside and fluttered about in the cream inspired by another.

Head dropping forward, hair hanging about her face in a veil of salt-crusted netting, she flushed. Warm and needy.

Fingers twisting in silent plea, the action familiar. As if she'd done it all her life.

With a hand on her nape, pinning her to the driftwood, he fucked her.

Fast.

Clumsy.

Letting the netting bite her skin, dragging against scales that hadn't broken the surface, he pushed into her on a wave of slick arousal he hadn't earned.

Hips rolling to meet inadequate thrusts, body screaming for more, Kore moaned.

Rasping and silent.

"Oh, fuck," he groaned, gripping her hips tighter. "Waiting for me, weren't you? Little cunt is singing for it."

Kore gagged, her throat raw. Voice gone. There was only desperate grief, and the longing for the touch of her monster.

Silent, shaking sobs wracked her body as the mortal bucked and grunted. His cock punching uselessly into her.

And then he came.

Short, pitiful jerk of his hips. Cock spewing a sip of seed that couldn't reach her womb.

But he didn't slow.

Stayed hard, kept rutting.

"Oh, shitte. By the gods," he rasped, "still so tight. Such a hungry slut. So good..."

Clawing at the netting, Kore bloodied her fingers. Empty and furious, her womb spasmed in search of something thicker.

But there was nothing.

Nothing but this sorry excuse of a man, with his watery, unworthy seed. A beast with sweaty skin and pale bravado.

Panting as he muttered, "You'll thank me, Siren. Sure as the tides," he gasped, fingers slipping against her skin. "I'll train ye up good. Give ye everything ye could ever want. Endless cock to feed such a hungry slit. You'll see. That's it, girlie. Such a good whore…"

Kore turned blackened eyes back. Pinning him with an ominous glare that reflected the silver moonlight.

Inhuman. Eyes meant for the deep.

He didn't notice. Blind to the threat, he pumped her with the sort of enthusiasm few might ever know. Indulging his wildest fantasies, crafting a tale few could believe as he worked himself into a foam.

And she saw it.

Moonlight shining on the crest of a towering wave.

Her eyes went wide as she tracked up, up, *up*.

Impossibly high.

And there, beneath the water's skin, she could hear the drums of war rushing in her direction.

The fisherman bucked against her, spearing her glittering pussy in shallow thrusts. Deaf to everything but the slap of skin on scales. "Take it," he groaned. "Take it all, you gorgeous fucking thing."

Hands fisting in her hair, he wrenched her head back as his cock kicked. "You're mine, beastie. All mine."

Pain sliced at the corner of Kore's jaw when he forced her head back. Blinding, suffocating anguish that saw her jaws gape wide around a breath she couldn't suck through her teeth.

The air grew heavy with the shadow looming over them. A dull roar humming through the night air.

Still, he didn't see it. Couldn't hear anything above his own selfish need. "That's it," he breathed, jerking and kicking inside her. "Gods, you're perfect."

Kore flailed, chest hollowing out around her stolen breath. The pain behind her ears almost enough to consume her.

But she didn't fight or thrash. Didn't move or plead or beg.

She twisted.

Looked back.

Watching the storm rise from the sea in a wall of glinting, silver fury.

And then… she smiled.

And it was dreadful.

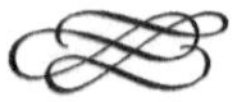

CHAPTER 22

She was gone.

The beach empty. The cave barren of any hint of life, except for the shallow pool swirling with the evidence of her rejection and the echoing hum of her absence.

Gills flaring in the stale air, Nyx paused. Seething, trying to catch even a whisper of her scent.

Gone.

She'd rinsed him out. Waited for low tide to give herself as much time as possible to put distance between them.

Clever little bitch.

He was almost impressed.

Sneering, he scowled at the tidal pool where his seed had been left to curdle.

Rejected.

He'd waited too long.

Tried to recover. To let the pressure in the trench stitch him back together until his gills could move freely, and his scales lay flat against blistered, tender flesh.

And in his absence, she'd been called to the sea—or taken. Her transformation nearly complete, while he'd fought the urge to resurface and drag Kore into the surf where she belonged. To stuff his knot inside that perfect, grasping slit at long last and pour the sea inside her womb.

Too long.

She was gone.

Her trail cold, already swallowed by the Black Sea.

The rage trembled in his chest, making the trident hum with a savage, dark power. The sort he hadn't touched for too long.

Lust for blood ignited in his veins, and with a preternatural grace, he slapped his tail into the tidal pool and turned black eyes toward the sea.

She'd refused his claim.

But the Black Sea was *his* domain—and she would give up her secrets when commanded to obey.

The resonance howled through his ribs, turning the sand liquid as he snaked from the cave, shot over the beach, and dove into the shallows with a grace that should have been forbidden outside of the waters from whence he'd come. Swallowed in a single gulp of slicing fins and ragged scales, he plunged into the sea that had allowed his bride passage.

Silence greeted him.

Oppressive. Whole.

Resistant, at first.

Pouring his wrath into the ancient weapon howling for carnage, he scoured the currents. Drew them through his gills and tasted the delicate ambrosia she'd left in her wake.

Faint. Diluted.

But unmistakably hers.

Slick.

Arousal thrummed through him, then, for Kore had given him a gift. The joy of a hunt.

Heart pounding with savage glee, he let his scales flare. Venting the heat kept close to his skin in preparation for the hunt.

"Flee if you must, little Siren." Dizzy with the rush, he laughed. A wicked booming sound that sent ripples washing ashore. "The tide will return what belongs to me."

The words echoed, a decree scrawled into the waves—carried forward as he turned his face into the current.

It was to be a hunt.

One she was wholly unequal to, his fledgling Siren.

Trident clenched in an unyielding fist, he flicked his tail and dove, but didn't descend into the deep. He coasted through the shallows, rich with oxygen, heavy with her scent. Tireless. A force cutting through the water with inhuman precision.

The little fool had tried to wash him away. Tried to mask her scent in the brine that called her to come, unaware how easily he could taste her. That she was in his every breath. The current rich with the flavor of a female in desperate need of service, for without him, his venom and seed—*his knot*—she would ache as she'd been conditioned to suffer.

Forever changed to need what only he might give.

And nothing could fill that void.

With every breath dragged over his gills, her scent grew stronger. Bolder.

Closer.

She was there. Floundering at the surface, the poor thing. Unaware of the gift he'd given, of what she would become when she accepted his knot and sank into the role he'd crafted for her.

Surging through her wake, he grinned. She was close.

The sea moved around him, giving up its secrets. Mirroring the fever in his blood. Giddy at the memory of her mouth, the grip of her divine cleft.

He surfaced.

Fins catching the current, holding him still, he blinked against the slap of cool, night air. Massive pupils reflecting the distant glimmer of stars and silvery blanket of moonlight as he searched for the girl he'd remade to suit his monstrous needs.

Wrapping him in ribbons of cold, the current sang through his gills.

But she was nowhere.

Her trail ended, as if she'd been dragged from the sea.

The realization sent a wave of frigid cold washing over him.

She was no longer in the water.

That glimmering trail of slick and blood ended, as if she'd been plucked from the waves.

As if she'd been claimed.

By another.

The moon hung heavy in the night sky, casting a silver glow upon the black waters. He scanned the horizon with eyes meant for the purest dark. A predator's gaze.

Still, there was no sign of her.

No hint of another *Pelagorn*—*Abyssari* or *Thalassari*—in the water who might have stolen her away, for she'd been plucked from the waves.

By a human.

A scream rang out.

Not the delicious sounds he'd pulled from her throat in the cave.

This was something else altogether.

Wet and broken, a desperate cry carried on the wind, but unmistakable in its haunting beauty.

A Siren's call.

Nyx shifted his grip on the trident, and he turned toward that glorious, devastating sound. And with a single, powerful stroke, he dove, propelling himself toward the distant shore.

It was the tide that betrayed him first.

Unnatural. A ripple where there should have been stillness. A shudder passed through the current, moving in the wrong direction.

She was there.

Bound in netting.

Bent over a log, her belly pressed to driftwood. Hair tangled and matted with sand that clung in clumps of soggy grit. Legs twisted together in a cruel mockery of a glorious *Pelagorn* tail, he watched the shimmer of new scales as her flesh jolted and rippled with obscene impact.

And behind her?

Driving a pathetic tendril between her legs, a short little cock rutting between swollen, glittering folds.

He saw it all in painful, cutting precision.

Her debasement at the hands of another.

Not a *Pelagorn*.

A man.

Eyes narrowed to slits, Nyx snarled and let his rage boil the tide. Kore, *his creation*, defiled by hands that reeked of rot.

She cried out again, calling to him through gills that had only just split her skin. Not yet healed. Gills that hadn't even tasted the sea before that grief-song spilled through the rift.

It was a haunting, dreadful melody born of pain and aching despair. It shook the water. Ached deep in his marrow. A keening so pure, it scraped at the edges of his soul and dragged a slurry of muddy anguish through his veins.

His every muscle tightened as he surfaced without a sound. Watching as her back arched when she braced against every thrust, helpless but to take it.

Every impact of flesh against scales twisted his wrath into a seething foam as her cunt swallowed something less than what it had been remade to take. Each shudder of jerking hips, each hiccuping, painful breath, one that would be repaid.

Nyxarion Korrides, first Sovereign of the Black Sea, raised his trident.

The sea responded.

Current twisting, the waves lifted at his command. Trident singing with the scream of old magic, he issued a call older than bone. Older than the kings of the deep or the open ocean.

It was a call to war.

The shaft vibrated in his grip, humming with an obsidian echo of the violence churning in his blood. Seething in time with the slapping squish of flesh on scale as his bride was rutted like day-old carrion.

It was a summons, an answer to every trespass man had made against the high seas.

He slammed the trident into the current... and hefted the three prongs into the air once more.

Drawing the poisonous waters up before sending them down.

Again.

And again.

Over and over and over, until he'd summoned a black wall of vengeance tipped in foaming white caps.

It rose from the deep.

Carried forward without wind or moon or tide, frothing and foaming. The messenger of a debt to be repaid.

It was wrath.

Retribution.

The man fucking his bride couldn't tear his greedy eyes from the stolen treasure milking his gummy little prick. Didn't have time to turn, or blink, or beg.

But she did.

Watching with wide, black eyes, her gaze traced the wall of water with something that tempered the rage squalling in Nyx's black heart, and fed it something... wicked.

And then she smiled.

It was the man's turn to scream, and he did it as the wave crested, washing away whatever sticky little squirt he'd managed to pump inside her before he was simply... gone.

Flesh peeled from bone.

A corpse tumbled through the unnatural current. Dragged down and broken, shredded across trees and rocks, mouth agape in an endless, eternal scream.

Tangled in netting, swept through the wave with a cry that made the black waters shiver and dance, Kore was liberated.

Gasping.

Bound.

The net pulled tight around her limbs—arms locked behind her, eyes wide, and hair a chaotic lashing halo. And her lips, they gaped wide open around a breath that couldn't come.

Helpless without him to guide her.

Held immobile where she was suspended. Afloat.

Weightless.

A drowned bride held aloft by the tide, tangled in her own foolish folly, naked and shimmering for his pleasure. Her throat arched, and she thrashed, legs flailing against inevitability.

Her death.

For her life as a human was over.

And her rebirth as a Siren?

Glistening skin speckled with scales that caught the light as the earth was washed away. Her eyes were wide, limbs slack, drifting as the wave swallowed her whole and let her fall.

Cutting through the surf, Nyxarion lashed at the current. Snaking through the carnage he'd summoned, fins stretched to sail through the turbulent waters, he rose.

Stretching one massive hand forward, the other on his trident, he claimed her. Tearing through the net with deadly claws, Nyxarion pulled her from its grasp and freed her from the trappings of humanity once and for all.

Head lolling, the girl was pliable in his grip.

Unconscious.

Her gills a seam beneath her jaw that did not flutter or gape.

Panic bubbled in his chest, then.

The flash of memory a cruel reminder of the bride he'd lost.

But the creature in his grip twitched. Still warm, heat radiating from gleaming skin in lazy pulses. Growing weaker, she was fading with every moment lost beneath the surface.

Drowning.

"No," Nyx snarled, straining not to boil the water around her. "I will not lose another."

Pressing his lips to those that were cold and slack, he forced a breath into her lungs. Thumb adding a gentle pressure to the seam where her gills were meant to filter oxygen from water.

And so he felt it when that flesh flickered. Weak, at first. A tremor unused to the never-ending work ahead.

Suspended in his grasp, Kore twitched.

Muscles lurching as she fought his claim to the very end.

He kissed her.

Tongue dipping inside, tasting her in his element at long last. Breathing for her, until those delicate slits behind her jaw shivered open. Wider.

And then she inhaled.

Water flooded her lungs.

Her pulse kicked beneath his claws, that stubborn flicker of resilience that had drawn him in, given new life in the heart of a Siren.

"Yield," he murmured, holding them in place as he cleansed her world and relieved her enemy of his pale life. "Open your eyes and sing for me, little Siren."

Her lips parted on a watery gasp. Blinking, she stared at her king with wide, shocked eyes.

"H-how?" she asked with the last breath of pure, wretched oxygen. It was a voice born for the trench. A voice laced with pain. Shame. Hunger and need.

"This ocean belongs to me," he said, clutching her delicate form to his chest. "And now, so do you."

Drowning was easier the second time.

The water didn't burn, not like before. There was no pain. Nothing like being crushed beneath the weight of a warship. Her legs ground into jelly, her hips shattered.

Drowning was…

Peaceful.

Terrifying.

A blend of cosmic horror and calm certainty.

That she deserved this. That she'd earned it.

She'd bled for sacred altars and unholy relics. Split herself on the pricks of priests, men, and monsters.

All for naught.

Because the gods couldn't be appeased through prayer *or* sacrifice. There was no amount of vestal blood that might spill to make them listen, no exact measure of human ashes that would be enough to save her.

Not from *him.*

This.

The water was heavy, pressing in from all sides, thick and suffocating as she turned bulging eyes up. Looking to the distant shimmer of silver moonlight.

Searching for an escape she knew didn't exist.

Not for her.

Not from this.

But she was held aloft, strong arms circling her waist. Inhuman arms thick enough to crush her ribs in a brutal embrace, strong enough to lift the sea and drown the earth.

Claws raked down her ribs as he held her to his chest.

Petting her.

Soothing the creature he'd claimed.

She shook her head.

A denial.

Unable to speak through the shock, she struggled against his grip. Pushing against the possessive circle of unyielding muscle.

She needed a breath! Fighting to get back to the surface, she kicked and thrashed. Lungs burning and full of water.

The beast bared his teeth in a savage grin. "Pretty little Siren," he tutted, enjoying her struggles against his monstrous form. His grip shifted, then. Claws trailing down her throat where they curled in a possessive necklace that reeked of scarcely restrained violence. "My most precious treasure."

His voice—it vibrated through the water, through *her*. A thing not heard, but felt. Deep in her bones, a hum turning her spine to liquid.

She gasped, inhaling a soggy breath. Lips parting on a soundless scream.

Bubbles.

They streamed from the slits in her throat, high at the corners of her jaw. Silver and fleeting as they escaped for the surface and left her sinking deeper... deeper...

Deeper...

Eyes growing wide, her hands flew to the seam where something unnatural fluttered and kicked.

Gills.

"Breathe," he commanded, and tilted her face down, forcing her to meet his impossible gaze.

Kore's lips parted, but no words came.

Because she couldn't speak.

Because she had no air.

A low rumbling chuckle shook his chest, and he clenched her tighter. "Ah," he hummed. "Sweet Kore. My living flame." He slid one hand down her back, curling his claws around the curve of her thigh, before he draped it around his hip. Abrading her inner thigh with the seam between flesh and scales. Man and Leviathan.

She thrashed, and his amusement only grew.

Laughing as if delighted by her resistance, he let his fingers slip between her legs. Taking liberties with a thing he owned. "You prayed to the deep," he crooned. "When no other wanted you, you begged to be broken across my cock. So break."

Between them, monstrous and alive, his cock emerged from his slit as if it knew it was being summoned. Long, ridged. *Burrowing.* Seeking entrance, the pearls already pulsing with vivid interest.

Mute, she thrashed despite the flames of need burning in her blood. Defiant. Utterly helpless.

"I am Nyxarion Korrides, first Sovereign King of the Black Sea," he murmured as the tip pressed inside. "And I am the tide meant to drown the flesh of the sun."

Shaking her head, bubbles streaming from her lips, her gills, in a frantic denial, Kore tried to beg.

"My voice the current," he added, fins flaring as the sea swirled around them, exposing the deadly barbs hidden within. "My venom the storm." Shivering, he flicked his tail and barbed her thigh, flooding her muscle with his toxin. "And my knot is the anchor that binds you to the sea—where you belong."

He swept his tail in a powerful arc and seated himself to the root in her clasping channel.

"I am the tsunami that fills your womb," he said and bullied his way inside with a deliberate, sinuous thrust. Stretching her open as they drifted through the current. "The toxin in your veins. The plea to the divine your gods refused to hear."

Back arching, Kore gasped. Gills flaring, her hands finding an anchor in his hair—her breath coming thin and shallow, but *enough*.

"I came when you were alone," he crooned, and cupped her face with the hand not fastened to the trident. "Found you hollow and made you whole. I am inside you now, my sweet Siren bride. My living flame. *Mine*," he snarled, and spiraled up. Lazy and powerful, despite the fervor of possessive lust driving his cock into her over and over again.

Pearls bumping over her clit, he dragged her over his length. Fucking into her at his leisure, forcing their pace to suit his needs.

"*This* is where you belong," he said, sinking deeper. "You cannot escape what you need. Cannot outswim what flows in your veins."

A shudder whirled through her. And, mouth hanging open, she let her head fall back. Starry eyes fixed to the surface as she was bred from below. Gasping as they sank into the abyss.

Together.

The water carried every sensation—the drag of his pearls against her clit, pulsing inside a cunt that had been remade to suit his whims. The scents she could taste. Sounds that echoed from everywhere and nowhere, all at once.

And the weight.

It was the water growing thick. Syrupy and noxious.

Crushing and heavy.

Her vision blurred as he dragged her down.

She whimpered, but the sound dissolved into a cloud of more damnable bubbles.

"You are *mine*," he rumbled, voice rattling her ribs as he

pummelled her womb. "You will break, and the sea will sing your name. So drown..."

He kissed her, then.

Lips sealing over hers, a claim was laid.

Lungs burning, head spinning, she grew stiff when he exhaled —sending a gush of ocean water to fill her lungs.

Clarity rushed through her brain, so he did it again.

And again.

Forcing her chest to expand, sending water rushing through her gills.

Breathing for her when the poisonous waters of the Black Sea threatened to smother her.

"That's it," he crooned against her lips. Tracing the seam of her mouth with his tongue. Tasting. "So good at taking me," he groaned, claws sliding up her thigh as he wrenched her legs apart and drew her closer. "My breath," he whispered, and his thumb found her clit, circling with a cruel sweep that drew her in. "My cock." He caught a nipple between his claws and twisted. "My seed and..." Trailing off, he took a fist full of her hair and forced her to watch when he withdrew, only to slide back inside. "And my spawn."

Kore tried to shake her head, but her pussy clenched.

"I'll keep you heavy with them. Breed you while you're nursing. Have you stuffed with seed until you can't remember anything but *this*." Drawing back, he stroked into her with his full strength. "The weight of my cock. The burn of my venom. The way your cunt sings when I breed you."

With a sob, Kore felt the fire spread through her veins. His venom. The sickness of her profane addiction.

Down they sank, carving a glowing trail in poisoned currents as the trident dragged them down.

And with each greedy thrust, Kore's muscles clamped around that invasive tunneling length. Lungs filled with the sea—with him. His breath. His venom.

Nyxarion.

The king of the Black Sea.

Her king.

Sustaining her as he used her, as the weight of the sea grew immense, crushing her ribs, he cupped the back of her head and pressed her cheek to his chest. The pressure built inside her skull, popping and crackling where it was trapped in her inner ears.

Still, he breathed for her. Forced her to acclimate as they drifted down.

"Look," he commanded, and pushed another breath through her lips.

She obeyed.

A yawning maw of endless night stretched below, and yet, amidst the gloom, a faint, familiar glow caught her gaze. Held it.

Blue.

Pulsing a soft welcome, outlining a structure that was both vast and uncanny.

"Behold," he rumbled, planting himself deep and pulling her inside out as he fucked her through the currents. "Vorynthar. The Seat of the Black Sea Throne. It shall be a new beginning. A rebel empire built in the dark."

Eyes wide, trying to take it all in, Kore watched as they drifted over the sprawling reef. Feeling it pulse with an alien heartbeat, she saw polyps dancing in the current. Waving as if in greeting to their king.

"Raskoril Coral," he said, strumming her clit. Forcing her to the edge of climax, only to fall back an instant before she peaked. "A symbiote feeding on the abyss, and in exchange"—he grunted, his rhythm growing fractured and jagged—"each exhale rich in oxygen that will transform my kingdom and tame the anoxic sea. One breath at a time. And soon," he said, returning his attention to her swollen cunt as his monstrous prick began to swell, stretching her wide around his girth. "Soon, this will be my throne, where you will break across my cock and grow heavy with my spawn."

Panic surged in Kore's heart, rising in perfect sync with the climax Nyxarion was forcing through her blood.

But she was trapped.

Impaled.

Hooked on an enormous bludgeon that grew fast against the mouth of her womb.

Claws digging into her tender skin, he held her steady as he forced her to yield, burrowing deeper. Always deeper.

"This reef will be a fortress," he said, and she felt him find his target. "It will feast on our enemies. Their bones will form the foundation of your nursery. Their flesh will nourish our young."

A shudder boiled her blood, as the cradle between her hips grew ravenous for his seed.

She came.

Mind flooded with horror. Body a swamp of everything she couldn't name.

"That's it, my bride," he snarled, stuffing her full. "Milk it. Let your body sing for me."

Head thrown back, Kore screamed.

It was a sound beyond hearing. An electric flame of ecstasy that clawed through her gills and burst through her lips in a cloud of frantic bubbles.

His cock pulsed. A living brand inside her.

Heaving, his pearls strumming her clit to prolong her climax, he followed her in ecstasy. Gushing, she was made to feel every ridge, every vein and pulsing bubble of lewd flesh.

"*Yesss,*" he groaned, scales lifting as cum poured into her. "Take every drop as you break over my knot. Let me seal it inside you, Kore. Your cunt remade as you become my bride. My Siren. The mother of my spawn. *Mine.*"

Her eyes rolled up, back. A second orgasm washed through her overwrought body.

It was blooming. Stretching her impossibly wide. A balloon of rock-hard flesh that sealed his cum inside her. Forced her to take what should have gushed into the sea.

Too much.

Too intense.

Spasming, helpless but to take as he overfilled his chalice, Kore milked his cock. Seed flooded her belly, bloating and round as he poured the tide inside.

"Such a good girl," he purred, chest rattling with that strange sound that turned her spine to jelly. Stroking her back as they sank into the heart of Vorynthar. "You're taking me so well. Almost halfway, my precious bride. Almost"—he pushed another breath through her lips—"almost ready to service your king."

The Raskoril coral throbbed in the dark, matching the jets of cum pushing Kore to the limit.

"Soon," he said, palming her swollen belly with a softness she hadn't thought might possibly exist on his rugged face. "Soon you will know nothing but this. The pleasure of being bred before the court. You will beg to take my knot, and we will drift through my kingdom for hours."

Convulsing in an orgasm that crashed one into the next, Kore broke as she was destined to do. Shattered beneath the weight of his words that settled across her shoulders. A mantle of destiny she was helpless to refute.

This was her future.

She was trapped in the abyss, forever bound to the beast who'd claimed her.

His captive bride.

Broodmare.

His... Siren.

Knot pulsing where her pussy was stretched bloodless and white, she felt another wave crash inside her womb. And she gasped. Resigned to it, now.

For there was no escape. No salvation or prayer strong enough to reel her up from the depths.

She floated, impaled on his knot. Ruined. Her wrists marked with net burn. Skin blemished from… everything else.

Clutched in Nyxarion's grasp, throbbing in the aftermath, Kore was limp. Swollen, her belly glowing with a bioluminescent hum that matched, she was grotesque.

Changed.

No longer something the sun could warm with that glorious radiance she'd been made to love.

She was meant for the deep.

Powerful tail propelling them through Vorynthar's skeleton, he drifted toward the seabed. Toward a structure she hadn't noticed until they slowed before it. Fins flaring to catch the current, he stopped.

Letting her look.

It was… horrific.

A cage of coral stood stark against the abyss. Glowing more intensely than anything else. Long spindles stood in a row, the bars of the cage arching in a delicate, morbid sweep.

"A sanctuary," he rumbled, and planted the trident into the sea floor, before he pushed another breath through her gills. Pausing to taste her with a lewd sweep of his tongue that shouldn't have brought heat into her cheeks, given that they were locked together. Her ribs heaving under the weight of what he'd dumped inside. "The Raskoril is dense here. Enough that you will be able to breathe as I build you a palace. Until your transformation has ended."

It was a prison.

One meant to keep her locked to the sea floor. Available at all times, caged to service his every unhinged whim.

Panic surged high at the back of her throat, leaking from the slits behind her jaw. Distant. Muted.

She was to be a doll.

A plaything trapped in a box at the bottom of the Black Sea. Mute. Helpless.

Nyxarion tutted, purring for her when she struggled. Making the liquid in her brain shiver, the cum in her belly heat as the venom in her veins quickened. Pussy bearing down upon his knot.

Slithering back, his cock slipped free. Uncoupling from her battered cunt, knot deflating in a gush of warm sperm. Leaving her gaping, ruined and sore. Slow when he reached between them to swirl two fingers through swollen flesh.

"This," he murmured gills flaring as the scent of her own slick drifted around them. "This is but a taste of what is to come, my sweet Siren."

Redoubling his effort to purr for her, he let the frequency deepen, sweeping her up, holding her close for a moment. And then, with something approaching reverence in his eyes, he cupped her distended belly. Heavy with the weight of his spend, hefting her girth, he leaned in to press a delicate kiss to her lips. "Soon, your body will know no other purpose but the joy you get from breeding for me."

Fins fluttering, he pushed her into the heart of the cage, and she watched, entranced as the coral parted. Clicking, crackling, crunching as the petals of her cage parted. Opening at Nyxarion's unspoken command.

"You'll be safe here," he said, raking his claws through the billowing layers of floating hair swirling around her nape. His massive pupils reflected the sinister glow lighting the deep. "My reef will nourish you. Make you strong enough to handle my brood when you are ready."

Kore shook her head. Daring to cling to his shoulders, her lips moving around a puff of silent bubbles—a plea that floated to the surface, unheard.

The glow cast an eerie shadow across the bars of her cage.

And for a moment, he paused. Head tilting as he considered the tiny female floating in his trap.

"You will be the mother of kings, Kore," he said at last, and shifted back.

The coral moved.

Folding around her.

Sluggish and disoriented, she reached. Tried to push it back, to claw her way free of the prison he'd built around her.

But her arms were weak. Her movements clumsy.

"Rest," he said, the word a low growl of possessive intent that, for a moment, made the coral pulse bright as she was sealed inside.

And then he was gone. A flick of his tail sent him shooting through the water.

Alone.

In a glowing coral prison that was both lifeline and tomb, the only thing keeping her alive, even as it held her hostage in the trench.

Hands pressed to the bars, Kore didn't bother trying to break through.

Not with a belly full of cum, skin stretched taut where she was monstrous and glowing.

Not without fins to propel herself through the current and outpace the monster who'd claimed her body and womb.

Not with a set of gills struggling to pull enough oxygen into her lungs.

There was only this.

The silent, endless weight of a city growing in the dark.

Kore didn't scream.

There was no one left who'd listen.

EPILOGUE

$\mathcal{N}$yx rose.

He knifed through the toxic water, the current splitting around him. He savored his triumph.

The reef blazed where it sprawled through the trench, a testament to his effort. Proof that his course was righteous. Claiming her—brutal, yet just.

And her.

Kore.

His Siren bride.

She was flawless. Adapting to her new environment at a speed he hadn't thought possible. She'd taken his knot and milked him dry. That clenching slit gulping down every gush pulse, he'd bred her placid. Kept her locked on his knot almost as long as he'd breed one of his own.

Half-curled around her belly, swaddled in Raskoril coral, Kore slept.

Not in the way of *Pelagorn*—who never truly rested—and no longer human. His Siren shimmered.

Dreaming.

Skin gleaming, veins of blue light traced her skin as her scales bloomed, and dainty, gossamer fins sprouted from her flesh. A mirror of her tainted *Pelagorn* blood. Almost vestigial, until her transformation was complete.

It sent a taboo thrill racing through his veins.

Eager to have her again when she woke, desperate. Addicted. Totally enslaved to his venom.

His seed.

His knot.

It was time.

Grinning, Nyx drew the conch from his belt, set it to his lips —and poured the black waters through those ancient spirals.

The call that burst forth rolled through the deep.

It was a summons.

To those still loyal to the lost *Abyssari* prince. Those who'd waited to see what he would make of his exile, and would rally behind him when they saw what he'd done to this human slip of a girl who *thrived* at the bottom of the Black Sea.

They would come.

Few, at first. Drawn in by the scent of a Siren. Eager for the scandal of that taboo creature who perfumed the currents from the Bosphorus to the Dardanelles—and beyond. A girl whose very existence broke the Accord of Nisyros, and promised war would come to the Black Sea.

But when they saw just what was growing in the deep, there would be many. An army of *Abyssari* would come to tend his reef as the heart of Vorynthar grew.

The call to arms quieted, and he turned back. Tucking his fins, he allowed himself to sink.

Ready for another taste of his bride.

Wakened by the conch, eyes wide and glittering with a delicious brand of fear, Kore floated in her cradle. Hands clutching the coral bars as a column of bubbles escaped her gills.

Mute, while she incubated.

Silent until she became fully his.

Nyxarion smiled, showing teeth. "There will be war," he said, and his cock pressed at the backside of his seam. "My army will come to witness my bride. And you, my stolen flame, will birth a new tide."

With a gesture, the coral wrapped her in a careful embrace. Holding her fast when his cock snaked free and readied her to service her king. Legs held open, bubbles escaping her plush lips, he slipped one hand through the bars and cupped her cheek.

"Soon," he rumbled, coiling his tail around the base of her cradle to anchor himself before he pressed inside that divine sheath. "Soon you will sing for me. And the seas will know what I have done."

Thalos would come.

Thalassari armies would flood the Black Sea.

But the high king would not find a meek and remorseful peasant pleading for safe harbor or leniency.

The birth of his dynasty had begun—and it would not come gently.

* * *

Pre-Orders for Books 2&3 Open Now

The sea remembers every sin.
The court has been summoned.
The open-ocean king is coming.

TIDE AND TEMPEST:
Book II of Song of the Black Sea

Pre-order now—before the tide rises on Janurary 31st 2026.

* * *

BRINE AND BONE (*Book III · Finale*)

The sea keeps what it's owed.

⟁ Pre-order this gripping conclusion to Song of the Black Sea
and be ready when the tide rises on April 30th, 2026

ALSO BY MYRA DANVERS

Swallowed by Darkness ~ **FREE**

- Grab your free copy of Swallowed by Darkness now!

The Last Tritan

- Flame to Frost: The Last Tritan, Book I
- Frost to Dust: The Last Tritan, Book II
- Dust to Smoke: The Last Tritan, Book III

Tritan Evolution

- Ravenous Innocence: Tritan Evolution, Book I
- Insatiable Corruption: Tritan Evolution, Book II
- Lavish Destruction: Tritan Evolution, Book III

The Feral Court

- Sinadim: The Feral Court, Book I
- Renegade: The Feral Court, Book II
- Giaus: The Feral Court, Book III
- Sickle: The Feral Court, Book IV

Atom and Evil

- Delirium: Atom and Evil, Book I

The Song of the Black Sea

- Seafoam and Shadow: Song of the Black Sea, Book I
- Tide and Tempest: Song of the Black Sea, Book II
- Brine and Bone: Song of the Black Sea, Book III

MYRA DANVERS

USA Today Bestselling author, Myra Danvers, is best known for her compelling mix of unique science fiction and dark fantasy worlds that feature feisty heroines, antihero men, and of course, proper villains. Though you may not always know who is who until the final pages…